THE ___

OF THE

HIGH FIELDS

RHIANNON A GRIST

LUNA NOVELLA #12

Luna
Press
PUBLISHING

www.lunapresspublishing.com
ISBN-13: 978-1-913387-89-1.

For the wild and wonderful coastline of South Wales.

For my very own Dylan ail Don.

Contents

One

The first time I saw the High Fields was in a dream. We all dreamed of it at one point or another. It was just the way of things in Severn's End. We blamed it on old fishing tales. Of the ships that were lost on the rocks or sung to their doom by mermaids or sirens or selkies. In my dream, I was on Abergafren Beach, grey sky above me, cold black sand beneath my bare feet. I walked into the water, pushing through the waves, sea creeping up over my thighs and my belly and my arms, deeper and deeper until my head submerged and I was walking through the gloom on the sea floor where the mouth of the Bristol Channel meets the Celtic Sea. Deep in the dark, I saw columns rising into columns, grey grass waving sluggishly as if turned by some unseen current, and the light—in colours I'd never seen before—twisting and inverting as if on hidden prisms, rang shimmering like some astral bell. In my childhood imagination, I thought it was magic. The power to bend the world. And for the longest time, there was nothing I wanted more.

Two

Grey water slapped the side of the boat. We bounced as we cut across the waves, sending a salty spray up and into our hair.

"We should go round. Cut across the waves," Corin shouted over the sound of the motor, squinting into the wind.

I shook my head and gripped the tiller handle tighter.

Trust me, I mouthed back at him.

I could alter the course, go with the waves, go round, but this is the only way. There's no going round with the High Fields. There's only through. Through the waves. Through the mist. No shortcuts. You have to fight the current to get there. The motor would handle it as long as I did.

The sky was grey.

Corin and his friend, I couldn't remember his name, sat looking out the front of the dinghy. They shared talk I couldn't hear over the wind and the motor. Corin's hair fluttered like a moth's wings. He turned a smile my way and I waved back, kicking myself for letting a pretty face turn my head like this. To think that was all it took to send me back.

I'd met Corin last night at the Severn's End Inn, one of the last old man pubs left since the pilgrims and the tourists settled in, and the only place a local like me could be left alone with her pint. At night, the coastline glittered with new bars, clubs and tourists shops up and down the newly constructed boardwalk, decorated with fairy lights, flags and flowers. New hotels were in the process of being built further inland, past the wide expanse of the dunes, so most visitors had to make do with the traditional fishermen's cottages and converted community buildings. Some of the older folks of Severn's End had managed to hold onto their small stone houses, doggedly attempting to go about their days as normal, dodging the out-of-towners. But more and more of the crouching, shrugging buildings were being made over for holiday rentals, turning the community of the town quite transient. Every day the small fishing town was taken over by tourists from all over, walking up and down the boardwalk, following tour guides, taking the haphazard and wholly inaccurate "History of the High Fields" ride built from the remains of the old ghost train in the now revived and reimagined Abergafren Fair, wandering through shops selling t-shirts, fridge magnets and phone covers saying "*Chase the Light*". Then, when the sun went down, hundreds of revellers took over the black beach each night, wearing flower crowns and submersing themselves in vats of cheap wine and fucking furiously on the cold pebbles, hoping to recreate the moonlit bacchanalia they imagined on the other side of the water.

This morning, the tourist crowds and the remnants of last night's shivering revellers had been beaten back by the unrelenting drizzle that came down in curtains of white noise, snaking in waves across the tossing surface of the sea. A small group gathered at the pier despite the rain, hoping to grab a photo of that famous glow on the horizon, to catch an air of that divine peace, inspiration, resurrection, destruction, whatever it was they were seeking, coming across on the wind. Sometimes you could smell incense, though that could have easily come from the multiple put-together shrines, with their tea lights and postcards and side plates of milk and bells and electronic musical boxes and fluttering petals, that dotted the volcanic rocks along the shore. When the rain cleared, many still would take a tour boat out onto the waves to get a closer look.

A few travellers each year would come here with a rowboat, dinghy or some other raft of their own creation and attempt to cross the sea to the promised shore, hoping their faith and determination would win them passage onto the High Fields themselves. I'd found where they shared their tips and advice online: The Queens Court Forum. I'd often considered shutting the site down, but the fascination was cute when it wasn't entirely based on falsehoods. Some of them claimed you had to build your boat yourself to pass, but Hazard and I hadn't done that. We'd rented ours. And who would know better than us? I even knew a few who had swum it. I remembered at least one from my time on the island. But that was… ten years ago? Had it really been ten years since I'd left the High Fields? How could a decade creep up on me like that? I supposed I'd become too used to the slow crawl of time in that unnatural place. Still, I'd had ten years to escape. I'd promised myself I'd head inland, start a new life in a landlocked city or on the top of a mountain, but I hadn't gone far since coming back ashore. I was still here, stuck in Severn's End, despite the tourists and the pilgrims, despite everything, clinging to this grey rock dotted with Christmas lights and hangovers.

"Have you ever met her?" Corin had asked me.

He had good hair, warm blond with a slight wave, and blue eyes with a ring of amber at the centre, like the penumbra of an eclipse. His voice lilted as he spoke, like his words were going up and down stairs and round corners, like his mouth was a house. His arms had a thickness and softness to them. The kind that said he'd never held an axe, but if he ever had to he'd have no problem splitting logs. He was younger than me, yes, but not annoyingly so, and he looked at me as if I was the only person in the room. That's probably why I let him take the empty bench in my booth. I even dropped my usual tactic of denial, of avoiding any connection between me and the High Fields. God help me, I wanted to impress him, like I was a teenager again. I wanted to make him stay and talk to me a little longer, until he saw whatever it was people saw in the people they want to keep around forever.

I smiled, coquettishly I hoped, and said, "Met her? I know her."

That's how we ended up out in the strait, bouncing along in my dinghy in the grey of the early morning before the tour boats started their daily orbit, salt on my lips, head a-tangle with too much drink, hope and regret. I was always learning new things about myself. That day I learned that I could sell out a friend for a chance at a pretty, young man.

Or perhaps that—even after ten years of promising myself I'd leave—I'd take any excuse to go back.

A flock of terns screeched high above us, battling against the wind as I urged the dinghy on against the tide, their calls rattling my aching head.

I would make it a quick visit. There was no harm in that. And I was only bringing two ashore with me, so the increased level of 'witness' would be manageable. The trip might even be pleasant. Check in on the new batch of the Faithful, catch up with Hazard, impress my young admirer, then back to shore. Yes. Everything would be fine.

"How long before we get there?" Corin's friend—what was his name? —shouted over the noise of the boat and the sea.

"Peter, that's not how it works," said Corin.

Peter, OK.

Corin explained that I was working to attract the High Fields to us through the use of higher vibrations, created through a strict paleo diet and a positive mindset. All hilariously wrong, of course, but his youthful confidence was so adorable I couldn't bring myself to correct him. Where did they get these ideas, I wondered. It was like listening to children explain Father Christmas or the Tooth Fairy or where babies came from. Sometimes it was better to let such innocent fancies be.

Peter frowned, looking between me and Corin, trying to figure out if he was pulling his leg no doubt. I was surprised to see him when I met Corin down at the harbour that morning. I didn't remember Corin mentioning a friend, but was too hungover to push the issue. Peter seemed Corin's exact opposite. He had a permanent frown line between his brows, and a head of dark curls with a sprinkling of greys peeking out from his temples. Thirties, I'd guessed, so more my age. Or perhaps a hard-lived twenties. He was wiry, quiet and observant; so different from Corin. If I hadn't met them together, I would never have placed them as friends. But then again, I suppose anyone might have said the same of me and Hazard back in the day. She was the centre of any room she was ever in, even before she became the Queen. Whereas I...

The waves turned sluggish and slow.

"We're getting close."

Three

Severn's End could have been a fairly prosperous port had it not been for the High Fields. The High Fields was, as we used to think back then, a strange patch of sea a few miles off the coast of Severn's End. Depending on the tide—or who came across it—it was either a deep sea trench filled with black water and grey weeds swaying for miles; or it was a swamp hidden just below the waves, catching inexperienced fisherman, running boats aground and wrecking the ships that tried to make harbour; or it was a marsh of wet mud and reeds, which would catch the sun somehow, or released some kind of swamp gas, creating the illusion of an ethereal, unnatural light that drew passing sailors in mad circles trying to find its source or drove them far from the water, never to attempt to sail out of Severn's End ever again. For most, it all seemed quite explainable. The shipwrecked cargo that never washed ashore was either blamed on the tides pulling everything further out to sea or the less virtuous members of the community making off with the most valuable of the flotsam and jetsam. Either way, the High Fields tripped up any attempt to make something out of the place, and whatever potential the port had was sapped away.

I'd always been drawn to the shore. Even back then, when Severn's End was just another forgotten town in the rural corners of Wales, poking out into the lonely sea. Most people in the area had the dreams, dreams of the water and what lay underneath, but I had a waking pull that would draw me to the beach to sit and stare out at the waves. It gave me a sense of peace, that no matter what happened here on the land—the unemployment, the crumbling services, my family turning in on itself, the chronic lack of faith in the fields and the people of this spit of land—there was always something bigger, bigger than all our problems. Why care about the latest trainers or whether your parents were going to fight tonight if the sea could literally rise up at any point and drown you all? In the face of those grey rolling tides, that eternal horizon, the endless crashing of the waves, any of the problems the land threw my way were wholly insignificant, washed away with salt water and the dead of a million years. When the other kids in Sunday School drew pictures of god, they drew an old white man or a sickly, pale Middle Eastern carpenter.

Me, I drew the ocean.

But as I got older, the ocean began to draw me too—quite literally— into its arms.

I started walking into the sea. I would walk, half-asleep, from my family's terraced house in the middle of the night, past the boarded-up town centre, through the fields, over the dunes and into the water. I couldn't explain why it felt right to be there, to be close to that power calling to me across the waves. The farther I went, the deeper I got, the stronger the desire would grow. Like if I could just kick off from the stony seabed and reach out my fingers, I could grasp it. The turning lights on hidden prisms. But then my mouth would fill with sea water and suddenly it would be wrong, so wrong, and the animal of my body would pull me frantically back to the surface, back to the shore.

My parents interacted with me even less than usual after the first time. They didn't take me to the doctors, as if by ignoring the problem *they could make my strange behaviour go away. Sometimes it was like they were frightened of me. Like they worried they might catch what I had. Like I was a monster.*

"Where is it?" Hazard used to ask in those early days of our friendship, before we took the leap, before she became the Queen, when we'd sit around a single use BBQ at the end of the dunes, wrapping ourselves against the wind that whipped off the sea.

I'd point out to the water, following the pull in my chest.

"There," I'd say without any doubt.

"That's where we'll go," Hazard said as we stared out over the waves. "We'll go to the High Fields."

Four

In the water beneath the boat, I could see grass. A field of fat, flat leaves waved dreamlike six feet under the dinghy, swaying with the grey tide. A stream of tiny bubbles trickled up to the surface. The memory came to me before I could stop it. Cold, soft flesh. A puckered mouth silent beneath the water. Then a mountain the colour of skin. The sound of tearing.

I turned away from the water and calmed my breath, pulse thrumming in my chest and my legs.

Now's not the time for that, I admonished myself, *get it together*.

The mists thinned, unveiling a wide marshland covered with the same grey-greenery from the seabed.

We had arrived.

"Is this it?" asked Peter, the frown line between his brows deepening.

He and Corin had been distracted by some discussion, tossing around ideas from the kind of books I should have been reading in university instead of the grimoires and manuscripts I'd found down in the library's special collection.

I didn't blame him for being unimpressed. The flat, marshy grassland spread as far as we could see in the white sea mist.

It would be easy to assume this was all there was to the High Fields. Sometimes this *was* all there was to the High Fields.

"C'mon," I said. "We've got to head further in."

"Is there more?"

"Maybe."

The boat slid from the water onto a slick grassy bank. I was careful on the dismount this time. It was easy to slide right back into the sea, here. I'd done it myself when Hazard and I had first taken the place. I'd ended up conducting that final part of the ritual shivering in sopping wet clothes.

I reached out to help Corin out of the dinghy. He gave me an odd look, as if I'd just offered him a live trout to swallow, then broke into a light-hearted chuckle. He high-fived my outstretched hand, gave me a winning smile, then gallantly leapt over the side of the boat all by himself. The tuft of grass he'd aimed for turned out to be far smaller and softer than he'd clearly thought. He stumbled slightly, righting himself before he could fall completely, but ended up knee-deep in brackish water. A flicker of a frown passed over his face like a passing cloud before he seemed to remember himself. He nodded at the water.

"You better watch out. It's tricky ground round here."

Peter, who'd quietly watched the whole thing, raised his eyebrows at me.

"Yeah, who'd have thought?" he said, then reached out for my still-waiting hand. I guided him onto the sturdiest looking mound of sea grass, boots squelching in the wet earth beneath our feet.

I turned to lead the way further inland, into the marsh.

"Are you sure it's that way?" Corin asked.

"Well…" I wasn't used to being questioned on these things. The Faithful always took anything I said, quite literally, as gospel. I supposed in the thick mist it would be hard to believe anyone could orient themselves. And it was probably good for me to experience a little more scrutiny. I'd seen how feeling you are beyond question could go to someone's head. But still…

"I *have* been here before—" I said.

"OK, OK," Corin put up his hands. "You know best."

"Sorry," said Peter. "We'll try not to ask any more stupid questions."

We trudged through the mist, heading deeper and deeper into the High Fields. Soon the grass turned to reeds. And then the reeds became saplings, bare and skinny like the legs of schoolkids or old women's fingers, fading in from ghostly shapes to stark dark lines in the pale mist. White cat tails and tight brown leaf buds dotted their dappled bark with a promise of what was to come. It was a little theatrical as an entrance. She must have known I was coming. The sea mist was cold on our faces, scattering a salty, dewy stardust over our hair and clothes. There was a growing sharpness to the air, reminiscent of the first bright day of spring, when the mornings still carry a thin crust of frost to cover the crocuses and turn the grass a pale shade of mint-green. It made me think of when my mother used to dye shredded coconut with green food colouring to make fake grass for cakes. As we ventured further, the saplings were exchanged for slightly more mature trees, cherry and apple, slowly covered in more and more blossom as we progressed, until everywhere we looked there was a canopy of pink and white taffeta ruffles, powdering the trees like a kabuki brush, filling the air with fluttering, delicately-scented confetti.

"It's like walking into fairy land," said Corin.

"Not a bad comparison," I said.

He was right. It was beautiful. It was heart-achingly beautiful. So beautiful I started to remember why I had stayed for so long. I felt an ache of homesickness for this place that threatened to dull the memory of what happened, the event that made me leave. I tried to drink in as much of the High Fields as I could, but every breath of that cold, fresh air was tainted by the sadness of knowing that at the end of today I would be leaving it again, or was soured by the niggling fear that I might end up staying too long and would never be able to escape again.

Peter pointed at a branch of cherry. "That's weird."

I leaned in to see what he was pointing at. A wasp of some kind was clinging on to the back of a snail. The wiry yellow body attached itself to the snail's large shell by the stinger— no wait—some other appendage.

"What's it doing?" asked Corin.

"That's a koinobiont wasp. It's ovipositing… ah… inserting its eggs in the snail," said Peter. "It's a parasite. It lays its eggs inside another insect and then its larvae feed off the host, slowly killing it until they burst out ready to start the cycle all over again."

"Through the shell?" Corin's eyebrows raised, barely crinkling his beautiful forehead.

Peter shrugged.

"They usually prey on caterpillars, not something as large as this. No idea how it's getting that stinger through shell though. Or what it's even doing here. This species is found in rainforests."

"Did you come along for a peek at the wildlife?" I asked.

I knew why Corin was here: to tell his mates he'd seen a real-life god, to grab a story he could dine out on for the rest of his golden life. But I still wasn't sure why Peter had come.

"Of a sort," he said. "You've lived here. What do you reckon it's doing here?"

"How many times do I have to tell you," said Corin, "it's here because this place is magic."

Peter pulled a face. I started us walking again before he could ask any more questions.

We clambered through the thickly growing wood and blossom, raising our knees to clear the long, lush grass, squeezing between boughs and branches that only ever seemed to squeeze tighter as we pressed into them. Just as I was wondering if we'd missed the Faithful's settlement, it appeared through the trees.

Two concentric circles of squat, round houses built from river rocks and thatched with reeds appeared in a small, shallow valley among the fruit trees. We'd reached the Hollow, the one and only settlement on the High Fields. Moss carpeted the ground between the stones of the paths, creating pebbled velvet carpets bordered with snowdrops, buttercups and daffodils. At the centre of the Hollow was the shared stone fireplace. Already a few of the Faithful were gathered round, making bread and stews for the whole village. I remembered roasting fish there on our first night, drunk on victory and the plum wine we'd grown and brewed that afternoon. From the colour of the stones it looked like the furnace had been expanded. Not much of an indicator in and of itself. Colours changed daily in the High Fields, but I'd never seen it happen with stones. The bands of discolouring created a tidal pattern stretching along the wide-mouthed front of the fireplace, as if it was yawning open.

"I thought there were only twelve people on the island," said Peter. "I've seen at least twenty so far. Plus, you've got thirty huts."

"Where'd you hear that? About there being only twelve?" I asked, immediately casting him a suspicious look. I'd learnt to always question assumptions about the High Fields— especially the ones that were correct.

Peter didn't reply, but I noticed him quietly tuck a notebook back into the pocket of his black bomber jacket. I didn't hound him. There were more pressing issues at hand. Namely the fact that he was right. There were more people, more huts, since I'd last been to the Hollow and, from the looks of the tools and piles of stones on the way in, they were building more.

The Hollow was expanding.

Oh Hazard, I thought to myself, *what are you up to?*

Five

The first time Hazard and I spoke was after the third I time tried to walk into the sea.

She was the *Angharad Evans, "Hazard" to her friends, "Hag" to her enemies, King of the Punks to everyone else, and once and future Queen of the High Fields. She was a tower of a girl, broad-shouldered and thick-limbed. Both immovable object and unstoppable force, she would have made a formidable rugby player had she cared to try. I'd always known her from afar, sitting in the back of the hall with a permanent scowl in infants, getting picked up by her nan from the headteacher's office in juniors, tucked round the back of the bus shelter with the other smokers in comprehensive. She was always surrounded by one group or another, laughing and grinning in a way that looked suspiciously like a snarl. She had that kind of magnetism even then, an aura that just made people want to be around her. Didn't matter if it was because they loved her or hated her. She just had a draw like that. Not bad for someone who lived with their nan. But even then, I could tell by her constantly wandering focus and rolled eyes that no matter who surrounded her they always seemed to bore her. By the time she came to me, she'd shrugged off everyone else Severn's End had to offer. Maybe that's why she'd come after the girl who'd washed up on the beach a third time. Maybe she was looking for someone who was drawn to something else, to find out what that was, to see what could possibly be more magnetic than herself.*

When I came to, coughing up a chestful of green sea water, I saw her perched on the crest of the dune above me. At first, I was grateful. She wasn't the police or the ambulance service or anyone who'd ask awkward questions about what I was doing in the sea. Then, I panicked. Of all people, why was she *here? I worried she would tell the rest of the school, spread stories about the weird girl who liked to walk into the sea, like that place could get any more miserable for me.*

"Why do you do it?" she asked.

I shrugged, not trusting anyone to understand, least of all her. But I should have known better. Hazard was always determined to be different.

"I heard there's something out there," she said. "More than mud and seaweed or whatever folk about town say. Something powerful."

I couldn't hide my piqued interest.

"You can feel it, can't you? The High Fields. You know it's real." She knelt down to me and reached out a hand. "Wanna find out what's really out there?"

I took her hand without a second thought. Finally, someone got it. Finally, someone understood.

Six

Squatting by the Hollow's fire, two older women were carefully arranging pebbles in a decorative pattern. Their loose tunics were knit from blossom and golden reeds, much like the clothing worn by the rest of the Faithful in the Hollow. More and more people wandered in and out of the small squat houses, exchanging small bouquets of apple flowers and sweeping blossom from the polished stones that marked the paths around the settlement. I ignored their curious glances and quickly took a headcount, my unease growing with the number.

The two women by the fire looked up as we approached. Their welcoming smiles widened into something more excited as they recognised me, their faces cracking with more and more wrinkles as if each line was a ray of joy shining from their eyes and mouths.

"Carys! Beloved! You came back!"

April and June, the last of the Faithful to arrive before I'd left. How could I have forgotten them? A proper wife and wife team, Hazard and I had called them 'The Months'. My gut knotted with guilt. They didn't know how hard I'd fought to keep them from this place. But here they were. Healthy. Happy. Perhaps I had worried over nothing.

The two women got to their feet and rushed over. I instinctively opened my arms to them and embraced both women at once. They had barely known me, but still I found myself gripping them to me like long-lost children.

June pushed back my hair. "You haven't aged a day."

"Lucky for some!" said April, to a scolding look from her wife.

"And new friends?" June looked over my shoulder.

Corin stood close behind me, smiling politely but distractedly. Peter, on the other hand, was off looking around the huts, notebook in hand like he was a building inspector here to sign off on the new construction.

"Hello, welcome," April cupped Corin's cheeks in her hands. "Got some handsome ones, didn't you? Come, we'll help you settle in."

Corin tossed his golden hair and laughed in faux embarrassment at the compliment, but once her back was turned he raised an eyebrow at me and pulled a face as if to say, *poor dear*. I frowned in reply, which swiftly went unnoticed. Under her quick kindness, April was sharp as glass. And Corin's speedy turn to belittlement had me questioning my judge of character. God, how much had I drunk last night?

"Ah, we're just here for a flying visit," I said, perhaps a little too quickly. "We'll all be heading back this afternoon."

April's smile faltered.

June squeezed my shoulder.

"You want to see *her*?"

"She's missed you," said April, suddenly, as if the words

had just burst from her.

June pressed her lips together, as if by tightening her own mouth she could help her wife anchor hers.

"How is she?" I asked.

June shared a look with April. "She's missed you."

We followed April and June up the moss-covered cobble path that took us up the side of the Mountain. When Hazard and I had first arrived, there'd been nothing but marshland. The Mountain was one of the first things she'd made, a tree-covered peak so we could look over the whole island and admire our handiwork. Her handiwork. A pyramid fit for a goddess.

Not like the *other* mountain to the north. A vision of flesh flared through my mind. Thankfully the trees blocked our view. I wondered if Hazard had grown them specially for that purpose. Or had she pushed that monstrous thing into the sea? I didn't know which option was worse.

Corin and Peter followed April and June along the silver stream that trickled down through the trees to the Hollow below. The stream rang along the pebbled riverbed like sleigh bells, the river stones shining like labradorite and moonstone. The water was alive with shimmering fish, and birds sang in the blossom-dusted branches that shaded us from the brightening sunshine. Either it was the warmth of the day, or the proximity to her, but as we climbed, the morning mists melted away, the leaves and petals lighting up like stained glass.

Corin's eyes gleamed with some deep satisfaction. He caught me looking at him and smiled in a way that made my thoughts trip over themselves. Peter was a different thing. His early shrewdness had fallen away, like he'd forgotten who he was. He looked up at the birds and the branches with a palpable awe, the sunlight catching and glittering the greys in the tight curls on his head. It was like watching children on Christmas morning, hanging on their every look of delight, as if their joy might banish the past and reignite my own sense of wonder.

But something else was bothering me. Something was off with the pattern of everything. Like it was the approximation of a forest, of a field, of a hill, but with some detail just a bit 'off'. Like a poorly observed painting where all the dimensions are out of alignment and multiple vanishing points draw the eye, crossing the leaves and the greenery with erratic lines of perspective. Like everything was fractured somewhere deep down. Nothing was growing normal. Not that anything grew normal here, where everything grew faster, lusher, more delicious, more vibrant. But this was different, even for the High Fields. A flash of translucent wings caught my eye. It was another one of those wasps. The iridescent panels on its wings were arranged in a strange pattern that seemed familiar. Before I could get a closer look, it darted away. Something felt wrong here.

I turned to June. "How have things been on the island? Any big changes since I left?"

April and June had arrived not long before I'd left, so their idea of what was 'normal' for this place would likely differ from mine a bit, but I wanted to get an idea if any of the Faithful were aware of something strange. Were they actually happy? Did they feel safe?

June smiled. "The sun rises, the trees blossom, the grass grows. There's plenty of crops and fish, more than we need.

We're warm, we're sheltered. There's no drama in the Hollow."

    She'd answered my question without any real answers.

    April darted a look back to us.

    "She—"

    "You can find out from the horse's mouth," June cut in.

    April nodded. "Yes, better you see for yourself."

Seven

My mother used to tell me off for not doing more to fit in. For not getting my hair cut into whatever style was fashionable. For not giving a shit about make-up and shoes and slumber parties and whatever the hell it was she thought I should have been doing as a young woman. Funnily enough she couldn't guide me into what that was. She'd never done any of those things herself, always instead wearing loose-fitting sweatshirts and hiding her face behind a godawful perm like she was trying to tuck herself away from view. But where she had deviated, she was now convinced I should conform, or great doom would follow.

"You've got to bend to the world," she said, "or the world will break you."

I told Hazard that once at one of our beach parties. Hazard threw the rum she'd snuck out of her nan's drinks cabinet into the fire, bottle still half-full, sending a small mushroom cloud up from the smashed glass.

"Fuck your mum!" she said. "The world should bend to us."

"What if it won't?"

We'd been discussing what would happen after school ended. All of our classmates were either making big plans to escape Severn's End or settling in to repeat the stories of their parents and their parents before them, keeping the town ticking over with just enough people to keep it a town. As much as school had felt like a prison, it had held us in a comfortable holding pattern. There had been no need to make big decisions or try to go anywhere or do anything grand. It had been its own kind of comfort. And soon that would end, and the adult world would want to take us and slot us into the merry-go-round, to continue the revolving machinations that kept money moving and buildings rising. And if we were not ready with an answer, no easily discernible slot for us to fit into, then there were going to be problems.

We'd spent the last two years facing school counsellor after school counsellor, telling us to make plans, pick subjects, start work experience for careers we had no idea about and, to be honest, we thought sounded perfectly awful. We felt as though we needed to present the world with a manifesto for the life we would try and lead after school, and if we failed to do so we would forfeit any future right to exist. Our contribution was demanded, otherwise we were a failed batch and should be thrown off the side to make room for better kids who were ready to get with the programme.

Perhaps if there hadn't been that pressure, we would never have come up with The Plan in the first place. Perhaps we would have just tumbled along through life until the right path found us or us it. But no, we felt we had to prove ourselves and at the same time revolt against the system of proving. Was it any wonder we chose to escape from it all?

Hazard leant against my shoulder. She was so close I could smell the spice of the rum on her breath.

"You know the story Mr Griffiths used to tell us?"

I nodded. Mr Griffiths had been our old PE teacher, a grim-faced man with a grey moustache and high blue shorts. When we'd taken our swimming lessons at the community pool, he'd impressed upon us how important it was that we did our best and learnt to swim properly. There was only the one pool in the county, so we'd hardly taken his warnings seriously, until the day he told us about how his father had almost drowned.

Mr Griffiths' father had been a fisherman, one of the few who knew how to traverse the strange waters around our coastline. On one occasion, the current had changed suddenly and sent him further out to sea than he'd originally planned. There the waves grew monstrous and tipped the boat, sending him into the water. Mr Griffiths' father was a strong swimmer, but the waves kept pushing him back under and his waterproofs pooled with sea water, pulling him further into the depths.

Water can take you suddenly, *he'd told the class.* It can go from mirrorlike calm to vengeful waves at a moment's notice. Even an indoor swimming pool deserves your respect.

"But did you ever hear the rest of that story?" asked Hazard.

"His dad managed to grab a tangled net trailing off the side of the boat and pulled himself up," I said.

"No, there's another bit before that. A bit he never told us."

I hadn't seen Mr Griffiths in years. I remembered there being some gossip about his father, that the old man had started leaving slippers in the oven and taking long walks to the shopping outlet outside town to look for his dead wife. Mr Griffiths eventually left the school to take care of his dad full-time and never returned.

However, one weekend when Hazard had been down The Tollhouse pub, the one place in town where the bar staff turned a blind eye to underage drinkers, she'd seen him tucked away in a corner with his husband, red-eyed and hunched over a pint. They were both dressed in black, like they'd come from a wake. Hazard listened in while she waited for the bathrooms—normally she would have just gone to the men's instead—and from their conversation she'd learnt that Mr Griffiths Snr had recently passed away.

As Mr Griffiths Jr took comfort from his drink and his husband, he talked about his father's last words before he sank out of consciousness. As the old man had swum in and out of lucidity, like a walker at night appearing and disappearing in orange pools of streetlight, he'd kept coming back to the time he'd almost drowned. He kept muttering about a light under the water, flickering behind pillars. A light that bent the world around it, stone becoming water, air becoming dust. As he got worse, he kept asking for that light. The nurses brought him lamps and torches, but he was adamant he wanted the light he'd seen in the sea. Mr Griffiths Jr said the old man wasn't entirely conscious of his worsening state, but he seemed to know he was ill and was convinced the light held some power that would make him well again. As the days passed, he became more irate, more frustrated that no one had brought the light to him, until one Sunday morning he looked to the corner of the room and his eyes widened.

There, it's there! he'd gasped, before slipping back into sleep.

He never woke up again.

Mr Griffiths' husband had consoled our old PE teacher, saying how the doctor thought it was a trick of the hypoxic brain, seeing flashing lights in the sea as his father had run out of air. That would explain why he'd seen it again towards the end, as his mind was slowly receding with the tides of time. But Hazard had other ideas.

"I keep hearing all these stories, and they all seem to say the same thing," she stood up from the fire and looked out to sea. "If there's some kind of power out there that can bend the world, I want it."

"And what if all the stories are wrong? What if the world won't bend?"

"Then we break it."

Hazard always knew how to make me smile. But time has a habit of casting the past in different colours. And in the shade of everything that's happened since, the thought that the world could be bent, let alone

broken, feels hubristic now to say the least.
   "I have a plan. Are you in?"
   Of course I was. She didn't even need to ask.

Eight

We reached a plateau on the Mountain's rise where the trees thinned out to a clearing around a gentle waterfall, flowing into a clear turquoise pool.

My part of the world—Wales, Pembrokeshire, Severn's End—is home to incredible natural beauty. When you got away from the closing car factories, the old coal mines and the abandoned suburbs falling into disrepair and discontent, you could find ancient oak forests, soaring valleys, golden coasts and river lands and rolling vistas like out of an Arcadian dream. But nothing back on land compared with this place. The High Fields was everything that was beautiful about my home across the water amplified. Over the years we'd taken what we'd loved about Wales and enshrined it here, given that beauty as a present to the island that would make all our dreams come true, that would be our home forever.

A shadow moved behind the waterfall. The water parted like a silk curtain around a perfectly round face lit up, not quite literally, by luminous green eyes.

Hazard, Queen of the High Fields, had awakened.

She stepped through the water, towering a good foot above

the heads of everyone else circling the pool. Curls cascaded over her bare shoulders, catching the cool and bright morning light like a halo. Her cheeks, round and shining, shone with an apple blush. With a stretch, she looked out over our small gathering, then upon catching a glance of me, she glowed. This time, literally.

The Queen pressed her hands together over her heart in a show of demure tenderness that shook me immediately.

"Carys," her voice rang in the air like a thousand tiny bells in a cave, her eyes welling up with glittering tears. "You came back."

Hazard would never have been caught dead performing this "American prom queen debutante bullshit", as she would have called it. She'd spent fifteen minutes ranting at me after she found out I'd once attended a daddy-daughter dance at the local church. It had almost ended our Teflon-coated friendship. She was a fighter. She was a bitch. She was the reigning queen and holy guru of a place that held no rhyme or reason. She was my best friend. She was not this.

She reached out her hands to me.

Of course, I went to her.

Concern cast aside and arms thrown round her yielding softness, her indomitable girth, my head rested on the arc of her breast as she gripped me with a tightness at once comforting and awe-inspiring. In the warmth of her embrace that seductive voice from earlier was louder than ever. Why had I ever left?

But I knew all too well why. I pulled away before the memory filled my ears with the sound of rupturing flesh and choking screams.

As I leaned away from her embrace, the Queen's eyes skirted over to my two stowaways. Her smile faltered. Peter gave a curt, cautious nod. Corin stood frozen to the spot, his jaw set in a rigid clench that caught me off guard.

"Who are these people?"

"Uh," I detached the guilt from me and let it sink into the dark. "These are some friends of mine. They wanted to meet you."

She gave them a smile then turned side on to me.

"They're supposed to take the trial by water. *Unaided.*" Her voice lowered to a hushed whisper.

We wrote many rules in the beginning. Some were easier to keep than others.

"I know," I whispered back. "They're only visiting. I'll take them back before dark."

She pursed her lips slightly, her eyes darting to them and back to me, then she broke out into another wide, warm smile.

"Any friend of Carys is a friend of mine."

"Thank you." Peter gave her a slight, deferential bow. "Your... it is 'Your Highness', correct?"

"If you wish," she laughed.

Peter made another note in his notebook.

Corin still stood frozen to the spot. I was beginning to worry the shock of the place had finally gotten to him, when he seemed to shake himself to and smiled that beautiful bashful smile.

"It's an absolute pleasure," he said.

I watched as she drank him in, clearly coming to the same conclusions I had. Her brazen look, this open devouring of him, left a little knot in my stomach. Hazard always could

have whoever she wanted, even before she ascended the High
Fields throne.

"I noticed you're building more houses," I said, more
to break her eye contact than anything else. But still, if
accusations of rule-breaking were going to be the first course
of our reunion then she had her own to answer for.

"Hmmm?"

I stepped closer and whispered.

"We're over the number we laid out."

"It's fine," she waved me off, but turned away from April,
June, Corin and Peter all the same. I followed.

"The witness," I said. "This is too much. Aren't you
worried about…?"

I didn't finish. I didn't even want to think of the other
mountain to the north of here, let alone say what had
happened.

"I have a plan," she said.

"A plan?"

"Yes," she said.

"Well, what is it?" I crossed my arms, "What do you need
this much witness for?"

She tilted her head.

"Why should I tell you? You don't live on the High Fields
anymore, remember. That was your choice."

My mouth went dry. She had a point, but I hadn't expected
her to be so blunt. It was good to see a bit of the old Hazard
still alive in there, but whatever reassurance I'd hoped to gain
I'd only found more concern in its place.

"In fact," she raised her head, magnificent with its
heady curls and sunny cheeks, "April, June, please have

everyone gather at the fire in the Hollow at noon. I have an announcement to make."

April and June bowed their heads and ushered us back toward the mossy cobblestone path.

"Announcement?" I frowned. "What's happening?"

"You'll just have to find out with the others, won't you?" She turned away from me and casually pointed a hand over my head toward Corin. "You."

He looked up, sending a shudder through his golden waves.

She smiled beatifically. "Stay for a while."

He smiled that handsome smile and walked past me toward her, as if I wasn't there. I stopped where I stood, wavering between the pool and the path.

"Oh, don't worry," she said. "I'll return him in one piece."

The clearing shimmered with a musical buzzing that made me think of iridescent wings. But before I could ask her about the wasp and the strange patterns in the High Fields, the light suddenly grew brilliant until I couldn't keep my eyes open anymore and I was forced back into the shade of the forest path, following April, June and Peter back down the mountainside. Shut out. Just like everyone else.

Nine

The first time we headed out, we were sixteen.

We hired a rowboat from one of the last remaining fishing businesses on the coast. A family-run enterprise, hanging on through the elder's long-held knowledge of the shellfish around the area and the junior's preternatural skill for finding a niche. They earned a crust driving vanloads of mussels to the restaurants in Cardiff, capitalising on local produce to out-of-towners. They didn't ask what we wanted the boat for, and we didn't tell them. Hazard rowed us out, the stronger of us, and I pointed where to head. It was a cool blue day with little wind and the water in the small tumbledown harbour was like glass. Perfect conditions for two teens with little experience of life on the waves despite living next door to them their whole lives. We'd actually packed bags, god bless us! Things we'd thought we'd need for our new lives in a place we'd only ever seen in our dreams. CD players, cheap rum and sleeping bags. Hazard had insisted on bringing this cushion decorated with a cross-stitch picture of a cat. I would have ripped the shit out of her for it, but I had an inkling her nan had made it. She'd spoken a bit about building a cottage on the High Fields for her nan to stay in after we'd settled. Just for visits, Hazard swore, because she'd be lonely now Hazard had moved out. I wasn't keen on guests, but that was an argument for another time.

Despite the blue beginnings of the day, as we got closer to that pull in my chest a haze rose out of the strait, blurring the edges of water and sky. The once-calm sea turned choppy, with waves that crashed straight into the front of the boat, pushing us backward.

"Just point where it is," said Hazard, words coming staccato between breaths, "and I'll find a way there."

I pointed the way the pull was telling me. We had been going in the right direction, but the waves were too choppy. We were scared the boat would tip and we'd be lost in the sea. Hazard turned the boat to row across the waves, trying to find a way around. But no matter which way she went or how hard she rowed, we made no headway. Eventually, skin gleaming and clothes wet-through with sweat, Hazard reluctantly handed me the oars and collapsed, panting into the back of the boat. I took over as best I could, desperately trying to find a way around, but soon the waves caught the bow and twisted us side-on to the tide until we were completely turned about. The sun went down, the air turned cold and for a paralysing moment we let ourselves drift in silence, unsure what to do next. After a few hours we bumped into the side of a fishing vessel belonging to the family who'd loaned us the boat in the first place.

"Thought you could just row out to it, did you?" the elder skipper chuckled round a drooping cigarette. "Thought you could just take it like one of Arawn's stags, and without so much as a knock or a shwmae first either."

Our faces must have broadcast our confusion at his mumblings, because he quickly scowled at us and spat the damp dregs of his fag in the sea.

"Uch, that's the problem with you lot. You've no respect for the old stories anymore. Well, Annwn has its rules," he stabbed a gnarled, nut-brown finger in our direction, "and you're no Pwyll."

"Alright, you mad bastard," Hazard huffed under her breath.

I, on the other hand, thought the mad bastard had a point.

We leaned on the railings of the tugboat and watched the patch of sea we'd circled for the last six hours shrink into the distance as we were brought back to shore. We didn't know the old stories. We hadn't even known there were *old stories.*

That needed to be rectified.

Ten

As we came back down the Mountain, the heavens opened and heavy sheets of spring rain drummed the leafy canopy above our heads and stripped the trees of their blossom. The mossy cobblestones were papered with wet petals and the branches grew fat with leaves. Peter was talking to April and June up ahead, but I barely caught anything they were saying. I was too lost in my thoughts.

Hazard had done that on purpose. She must have known how I'd taken a shine to Corin. That's why she picked him. She'd meant to hurt me. Like I had hurt her by leaving. I was less fussed about losing Corin and more bothered by the fact that she would so casually take him. It was within her power. Her right. But I'd thought I was exempt from all that. I thought I was the exception to her reach. Maybe I never had been. Maybe it just took ten years for me to see it.

Well, I was under no such illusion anymore.

I wanted to go. As soon as lunch was over, I was going to take the dinghy, grab Peter and Corin—if Corin even wanted to leave—and I was getting out of here. I was leaving for real this time. Away from the High Fields. Away from Abergafren and Severn's End. Away from Wales.

By the time we arrived back in the Hollow, blue sky appeared in patches between white clouds, the cherry trees were green and the wisteria had bloomed, covering each of the stone huts with lilac tears. The rest of the Faithful were clearing up breakfast. I was surprised none of them had offered us anything to eat. It was uncharacteristically rude for the Hollow. Perhaps Hazard had sent word, to humble me no doubt. No worries. We'd eat when we got back to shore. I decided to let Peter in on my new itinerary for the day, but when I looked for him, he had disappeared. I rubbed my temples in frustration. *Oh god, not another one.*

I walked over to the fire pit, where June was braiding daisies into April's hair.

"Where's—?"

"Probably chatting with the others," said June, raising an eyebrow. "He's a 'friendly' one. Full of questions."

The tone of her voice told me I was right not to like the sound of that.

"What kind of questions?"

"Well, last thing he asked me was where the bathrooms were," said April.

"Right. Are they still—?" I asked.

"Next to the rust stream, yes. Are you alright? You look a little—"

I walked away before she finished speaking. It was rude of me, but I was tired of being kept out of the loop. First Hazard had gone out of her way to embarrass me. Now the guests I had so kindly brought here were wandering off, like I was nothing but the ferryman. Well, they didn't know this place like I did. No one did. Maybe not even Hazard.

I marched down to the stream. It was the same one that flowed from Hazard's mountain pool, cutting through the centre of the Hollow to provide the Faithful with clean drinking water. That had been my idea. At the edge of the second ring of stone houses the stream split into three. First the amber tributary where the water met a small collection of hot springs. Here there was a series of small pools, shaded by reed walls, where the Faithful could bathe. Second, there was the black stream where the water was soft and the riverbed full of good-sized dark river rocks, perfect for washing clothes and tools. Then third, there was the rust stream bordered with a series of small huts where the Faithful could defecate and urinate and let their bodies do what they needed to do.

I found Peter standing by the edge of the water, where the stream split into three. He looked back at me at the sound of my approach and waved me over.

"Look," he pointed at where the stream changed into the three different coloured waterways. "How does it change colour like that?"

I sighed. He was surprisingly easy to impress. It would be endearing if I wasn't so angry.

"High Fields," I shrugged. "Her Highness can make the world however she wants it here. You should see the toilets."

He laughed. It was a genuine laugh, a delighted laugh. Unintentional, like a bubble rising up from deep within and popping out of his mouth before he could stop it. I was envious of it. God, to have that feeling again...

Peter pulled out his phone and opened up the camera app. Without a second thought, I knocked it out of his hand.

The reflex had never left me.

"Hey—"

"You can't take pictures. It…" how could I explain this to tourists? "People seeing things from the island, noticing its strangeness, it magnifies the power of this place—her power—somehow." I picked up his phone and handed it back to him. "We call it "witness". Individual people turning up on the High Fields are like, we're like logs on a fire. We burn nice and slow. Plenty of fuel, but controllable. You start taking photos, recording video and sharing that with the wider world, and the witness quickly gets out of control. One photo gets thousands of views and it's like…"

"Pouring petrol on a fire?"

"Dumping fireworks on a fire," I said. "We had a photo get back to the mainland once and…" I didn't want to go into what happened.

Peter's face turned suddenly shrewd again, sharp and seeing. "Is that why you left?"

This was less cute.

"OK, tour's over. We're heading back to the boat."

"That's a bit soon, don't you think? What about the Queen's announcement? Back on the Mountain, she said there was going to be an announcement."

"I don't care," I said.

"It sounded important. Shame to come all this way and not know."

"She's the Queen. Every announcement is important. We're leaving."

He sighed and pulled a folded wallet out of his pocket. No, not a wallet. A badge.

"I'm detective Peter Jenkins."

I blinked stupidly.

"Police aren't supposed—"

"I know," he said. "Normally we wouldn't interfere, but—"

"Why are you telling me this? Do you have any idea—?" This was bad. Very, very bad. Police on the island, and I had brought them. I grabbed his arm. "You have to go."

He shrugged me off, easily, confidently.

"We've had reports of missing people. Last time they were seen, they were heading out to this island."

"People have a right to go missing," I said.

"And I wasn't going to force anyone to come back. I came here to make a wellness check. See that the missing people are safe and happy in this… this place, and then close some cases. So, imagine my consternation when I arrive and there's no sign of the missing people anywhere."

Shit. The notebook. The questions about the Faithful. I'd even seen him poking his nose around the Hollow. I'd been too busy sulking over Hazard and Corin to pay attention.

"So now I'm having to be a bit more forthcoming, because I get the impression you're a little more switched on than most folk on this island."

Another more pressing thought came to mind.

"Is Corin—?"

Peter shook his head. "I found him online on The Queen's Court Forum. You know there's a pinned thread sharing theories on how to get onto the island, right? Without passing the… what did you call it? The water test?"

That bloody forum. I knew I should have had it shut down.

"Corin was looking for a way to get here?"

"Yes. Didn't you know? That's the whole reason he came." Peter waved a hand back toward the Hollow. "He's into all this. A believer. I think he tried to cross before, but it didn't work." Peter shook his head with a small, bemused chuckle, "You really didn't know? He's all over that forum. Christ, some of his posts—what was it he wrote?" He flicked through his notebook. "Ah, here. 'As men, we are raised to strive for greatness. But how can you be great when the universe, when time, dwarfs you, buries you in its sheer scale?' Here's one you'll like: 'Some men spend their whole lives and fortunes striving for the kind of fame or infamy that will last beyond their paltry lifespan. And yet some nobody burger flipper managed to achieve godhood. The universe certainly has a sense of humour.'"

Corin had cheated his way here. And I'd let him. Foolish woman. I knew I'd been falling for a scam of some kind.

"He was asking after someone at Severn's End. Rumour was, there was someone who could get us onto the island. Someone who'd already passed the test, but didn't live in the High Fields anymore. I offered to team up with him, give us a better chance of finding the right contact. Didn't take as long as I thought it would, but then again, he is very pretty."

My blood burned hot in my face.

Peter turned his phone to me and swiped through a series of photos.

"Now I've been honest with you, perhaps you can do the same for me. These are the people I'm looking for. Do you recognise any of them?"

I briefly glanced at their faces and looked away. Flashes of flesh went through my mind. The screams, the splitting skin. I couldn't bear to look at them, happy and healthy, before they ever heard of this place. I shook my head.

"Sorry," I said.

A look of disappointment washed over Peter's face. "Are you sure? Could you look again for me?"

That was the last thing I wanted to do.

"I've not seen these people before. Maybe they came after I left."

"Hmmm," Peter nodded. He made a note in his notebook and put it back in his jacket.

"Look, Carys, I'm stumped, and I don't like feeling stumped. In my experience it usually means someone's up to no good. You and the Queen have a connection. Perhaps you can find out from her what's been going on here?"

I didn't want to tell him my concerns, about how the High Fields seemed... more... this time. But he was right. I had to talk to the Queen.

Alone.

Eleven

The fisherman's words stayed with me long after our return to shore.

You're no Pwyll.

But what was a pwyll? Or "poo-ell", as I'd wrongly transcribed over and over in my school diary.

I checked the school library first. Hazard would not own up to knowing me, not in school, not in front of her hangers-on, so I had to go alone. Our school had a comprehensive collection of Roald Dahl, Judy Blume and Jaqueline Wilson, spread between intimidating tomes of the compulsory classics, tucked into the walls of a square room to the side of the assembly hall. The word sounded Welsh, so I checked the Welsh dictionary, but thanks to my poor spelling I didn't find anything. I asked the librarian, but she was young and from Liverpool and didn't know what I was talking about. She kindly suggested that I ask our Welsh teacher instead.

It was towards the end of the year and instead of revising for exams, I'd focused all my attention on getting to the High Fields. Neither of us had made much effort in our Welsh classes—compulsory up to the age of sixteen—until now. My teacher was surprised to see me in his revision class. He was even more surprised when one of his most apathetic students started asking questions about key characters from the first branch of The Mabinogion.

At risk of me taking over a class on mutations, he handed me a battered copy from the classroom's little Welsh library and sent me to the back of the room. I'd heard of The Mabinogion *before, seen it with its illustrated cover of Celtic knots twisting over and into each other like an intricate infinity symbol. But I'd never realised how important it was to our goal. Wales has its own lost mythology, passed down over thousands of years by specially-trained bards, tweaking and changing the stories with each new generation. There had been so many tellings over so many years it was impossible to tell who first composed them or even when. And at the very start of those stories was the tale of Pwyll and his encounter with Arawn, the king of Annwn.*

The Other World. A land of miracles.

The gist of the story was that, while out hunting, Pwyll got separated from his party and came upon a stag being hounded by white dogs with red ears. He chased them off and put his own dogs onto the stag. Trouble was the white dogs, and therefore the stag, had belonged to Arawn—a powerful king, an immortal sorcerer or an ancient god depending on which historical records you read. What Pwyll had done was akin to stealing from Odin or Hades. As an act of atonement, Arawn suggested Pwyll take his place for a year in Annwn and kill Arawn's rival for the throne. Pwyll agreed to the exchange, and entered a world full of wonders. What was more, Pwyll was chieftain of Dyfed—the old name for Pembrokeshire, the area where Severn's End resided.

When I showed the book to Hazard after class, she gave me a wide-eyed look. Could the story of Pwyll really be about the High Fields?

We spent most of that evening on Abergafren Beach, reading and rereading. The thought that there could be hidden wonders in our ignored corner of the world excited us. We both religiously attended every Welsh revision class after that. We wrote to the headmaster to allow us into sixth form despite our late application. Surprised by our sudden zeal for learning, and perhaps influenced by the concurrent political push for education, she accepted us as long as we made the grades. I don't think either of us had ever studied as hard in our lives.

We both scraped Cs and hastily made new plans, including a lot more studying than we'd originally thought. Specifically, History, English Literature and Welsh. If Annwn had rules, then perhaps so did the High Fields. Maybe the past would give us the rulebook.

The only thing standing in our way was the thin offering of Welsh mythology and ancient history in the school library. There was an abridged and illustrated copy of The Mabinogion *and a Welsh-language version of the* Tales of Taliesin, *but not much else. We asked our Welsh teacher where we could find more stories, older ones, untainted by retellings. He gulped at us like a goldfish, lost for answers.*

"Well, erm, I don't know, girls. But that would make a fun project!"

He could teach us conjugations and syntax, but nothing about the origins of our language, our stories. We'd have go digging somewhere else. We tried the Severn's End library, but it mostly catered to baby groups, kids sneaking passages from Stephen King while their parents browsed the Beatrix Potter, pensioners browsing the Jackie Collins, students looking for a quiet place to study and folks using the computers. It wasn't really the place for hunting down ancient manuscripts and tomes like we'd seen on Buffy the Vampire Slayer. *We were lost.*

Until one lunchtime, while mitching off English on Abergafren Beach, Hazard discovered referencing.

"Hey, there's a bit at the front," Hazard threw the book to me, spine now bent and pages folded. "Read the introduction."

It had never occurred to us to read anything other than the main bits of a book before. I knocked black sand out of the pages and took a look.

'The Mabinogion *was first translated into English by Lady Charlotte E Guest between 1837 and 1845 from the* Llyfr Coch

Hergest *or* The Red Book of Herghest—"

A breakthrough. At last!

Hazard raised her fists in triumph.

I read on and my smile faded.

"—a fourteenth-century manuscript currently part of the collection at Jesus College, Oxford."

Hazard lowered her arms. We sat in silence for a moment.

"So how do we get to it?"

"They're not going to let two randos at a rare manuscript," I said. "You'd need to be a researcher or a student or something."

"OK, what grades do we need to get into Oxford?" she asked.

I had to admire her confidence.

"It's not just grades," I said.

Hazard frowned. "What else would you need?"

"I think you have to understand politics and economics and Latin and know which fork to use first at—"

"Alright, alright. I get the picture. What if we just asked them nicely?"

"You? Ask nicely?"

"Shut up." She kicked sand my way.

I scanned the rest of the introduction.

"Wait, here's something." I shuffled next to her, "Though some claim The Red Book *is the oldest written copy of the Mabinogi,* The Llyfr Gwyn Rhydderch *or* The White Book of Rhydderch *predates it by several decades and may even have been The Red Book's exemplar…"*

Hazard crossed her arms.

"So where's that one? Cambridge?"

I flicked to the back and checked the references. I stopped and smiled.

"The National Library of Wales."

"Cardiff?"

"No, Aberystwyth," I said. "And they have a university."
"Do you have to understand politics and fancy forks for that one?"
"No. I think that one's just good grades."
Hazard nodded.
"OK, Aberystwyth it is then."

At seventeen, Hazard and I put the University of Aberystwyth down on our application forms. The old seat of learning sat on the west coast of Wales, overlooking the grey sea some way north of where I felt the High Fields calling. The university town was an insulated bubble away from the world, with the National Library of Wales right on its doorstep, a deposit library holding a copy of every book published, maps, archives and arguably the first written manuscript of The Mabinogion. *If the history of the High Fields was written anywhere, we were sure it would be found there.*

We didn't even bother picking a second choice. It was Aberystwyth or bust.

So, when I got into Aberystwyth and Hazard didn't, it nearly threatened to put the whole endeavour on hold. Hazard tore up her rejection letter and threw it into the sea, screaming obscenities to the High Fields somewhere out there beyond the waves. I could understand her frustration. My grades had always been alright, but I'd never shown much interest in anything beyond the beach and its stones and the sea beyond. Somehow, the admissions board must have caught a spark of something in my personal essay they hadn't in Hazard's.

"What did you write in your essay?"
"I can't remember."
"Think!"
"I don't know!"

Hazard screamed into the night air. She kicked sand, sending up less sand than I knew she would like, making her kick harder and harder, frustrated at the lack of evidence of her felt power and strength in the world. She wasn't alone in her disappointment. As much as Severn's End had been an inhospitable place for strange girls like me, the thought of moving away alone terrified me. Once she'd calmed down and we'd been silent for a good while, I spoke up.

"Come with me."

"They're not going to let me stay in your poncey student halls!"

"We'll rent a place. Our own place. I'll take you into the library with me. I'll share everything I learn. We could double up the work. Get through the uni stuff quicker and leave more time for research."

She thought it over as the waves lapped quietly in front of us.

"I'll want half your degree."

"I'll give it to you."

Twelve

By lunchtime, the canopies were fat and full like in early summer back on the mainland. I used to look at the trees after weeks of rain and sunshine, and wonder how I forgot they could ever be so green. It was almost monstrous how the colour took over the land again, replacing the brown bracken and the copper ferns of the hillsides, chasing out the long, wet winter with brilliant, verdant summer. Life would not be contained. Even the barest, deadest rock would soon be teeming with moss and lichen. The High Fields was summer tenfold, abundant and indomitable.

The coolness that came with the midmorning rain was already a memory as the midday sun now burned off the mists that had draped themselves over the shore and the Hollow and lit up the sky until it was white-hot. It was a bright heat, the kind that tightens the skin and robs the air from your lungs. Why had Hazard made it so hot? I sat in the shrinking shade of one the cherry trees, watching Peter through my eyelashes and the glare of the sun as he talked with more of the Faithful. He had his act down well. Snobbish cynic turned childlike enthusiast. Irresistible. He must have known I was watching him. He must have known I wouldn't dare share his secret. Admit to bringing the pigs to the High Fields. That was one of the first rules. No police. You let them in, you let in the power of the mainland. Not even I would be immune to the Queen's wrath. The heat rose and the hairs on my arms felt crisp. I was regretting returning more and more by the second

I felt her coming before I saw her. I always did.

Trees creaked with the sudden weight of new leaves as grass rustled up out of the ground like a peacock shaking its feathers. Tree roots erupted out of the dirt like veins and the air turned thick with pollen until it shone as if littered with spun gold. The sunlight flared white, the glare bleaching everything in sight. The Faithful gasped with joy. I frowned and covered my eyes. She was getting more theatrical.

Her Highness appeared in a swirl of iridescent flame in the centre of the Hollow, ribbons of citrus-scented smoke snaking through her fingers while rays of sunlight glinted off her mane of curls like a crown. Her arms were raised in the air as if she were holding up the sky itself.

"My friends," she said.

The Faithful shuffled round, reaching for her arms. April blew kisses as June gave her wife an affectionate squeeze.

A voice from the crowd called, "Mother!" I flinched. For a moment I thought Her Highness did as well. But she just smiled beatifically at her loving Faithful. A sea of hands raised in her direction, voices calling for her, sending her love.

I almost didn't see Corin stood at her side.

It threw me, him standing there, immediately in a place of such trust and intimacy. After a morning? How quickly he'd forgotten me. Looked like Peter was right. He'd just used me to get to the High Fields, to get to her. She towered over him, statuesque like a Valkyrie, but you wouldn't have guessed who was the god and who was the follower by the way he gripped her waist. He stood gazing down on the Faithful with an air of authority, his eyebrows arched and his eyelids heavy as if weighing up the people stood before him, his mouth turned up slightly at the corners in a self-satisfied smile, already looking like he ran the place. I was surprised that Her Highness would put up with that. Though the way she seemed to pointedly ignore me made me think there was more to this than Corin's charm and good looks. This was a message. This was me being put in my place. This was Her Highness letting me know how easily I could be forgotten. How easily I could be replaced.

After all these years, after everything we went through together, I still feel like I'm just keeping the seat warm for someone else.

Out of the corner of my eye I saw Peter cross his arms and tilt his head.

"I am so glad to have my dear Carys back amongst us again."

Love wafted back to me from the crowd. Surprised, I waved, never quite comfortable with the limelight. Perhaps I'd been wrong about her. Maybe she'd just learnt how to get on without me. Was that really her fault? I felt hideous for thinking she'd forget me, an ugly, tied-up feeling where you feel wronged and wrong all at once. Perhaps I'd been petty? I didn't like this. I wanted to head back. I wanted to leave. But after Peter's warning, I knew I needed to find some way to get Her Highness on side. Perhaps with her power we could create a convincing enough ruse. At least get our stories straight. I knew what I had to do, but all I wanted was to run away.

But Hazard had another surprise waiting for me.

"I have exciting news for you."

She reached back for Corin's hand. I stepped away from the tree trunk.

"We have exciting news for you."

I straightened up.

The Queen of the High Fields folded back her voluminous skirts, revealing her swollen belly. My mouth fell open. The Faithful gasped with joy. Peter shot me a confused look.

"Soon our light will grow and we will take our message into all the world. We will spread our light throughout space and time."

Her Highness cradled her belly, that beatific smile spreading across her literally glowing cheeks. Fear ran cold through me. How could she do this? After what happened, after what I had to do for us, how?

"This, what we're doing here, it isn't about me," she said. "Who I am isn't important. It's what I am that matters. I'm a filter, a prism. All of creation, all of existence, including yourself, emits this beautiful light. And I take in that light, and I pull it together. I refract it into its constituent parts. Then I reflect it back to you," she smiled. "In short, this is all you."

She raised her hands in the air as that strange light emanated straight out of her, like a hidden cloud had passed or the sun had suddenly chosen to rise just behind her.

"This is all you!"

The first row felt it first, then the next two rows, then the four behind, as an invisible wave rolled through the Faithful. The crowd burst into rapturous applause, whooping and cheering.

Some people near the back were crying. Others closer to the front fell to the floor, shaking and laughing with some alien joy. Some of the Faithful waved flags and danced with ribbons as others shook their arms in the air, tongues ringing with new songs and languages never heard before, as an unspeakable joy rolled over the crowd like a slow-moving tidal wave.

I felt the pull, strong and insistent, like a fishhook in the centre of my chest, drawing me toward the singing crowd, washing the fear of that swollen belly right out of me. The strength of it took me by surprise. My head swam and my heart ached, like a longing for a lover or a long-lost home now in reach. It radiated through my arms and my legs, practically orgasmic, with a bittersweet tang of grief. I was simultaneously overjoyed to be in that moment and overcome with loss because I knew it would end. The urge to sob and laugh fought over my senses, while other members of the Faithful collapsed under the thrall. They rolled on the ground, swinging back and forth between sorrow and joy, wails and full-throated laughter bubbling up from their wide, pink mouths. I managed to back further away into the trees, pressing my fingernails into the palms of my hands to bring me to my senses. Across the clearing I saw Peter similarly staggering backwards, clutching his chest, tears trickling down his cheeks. He caught me looking, turned away and wiped his eyes.

The pull was strong. Stronger than I'd ever felt it before. I gripped the bark of the tree behind me, eyes caught on Her Highness' belly. Fear scratched away at the base of my spine once more.

Was this her big plan? What was she thinking?

Thirteen

As the day came closer to the move to Aberystwyth, Hazard became strangely reluctant.

"It's in the middle of nowhere."

"It looks shit and grey and miserable."

"I don't get why we can't just study from Severn's End."

"I thought you hated Severn's End," I told her.

She punched me in the arm and told me to shut up.

I had an idea of why she was reluctant, so I showed her a train timetable and pointed out the pensioner's discount for her nan.

"God," she said. "How old do you think I am, mun!"

But she brightened again on The Plan after that.

Hazard followed me north. In between introductory classes, I helped her apply for an apprenticeship at a nearby nature park. It was a pretty patch of woodland, home to bluebells and daffodils and gorse, spread over the hillsides between the seaside university town and an old quarry. While I learnt how to use the library, sift through material and decide what was useful and what was not, she learned how to maintain forest trails, build handrails and use a chainsaw. Considering the job was just a stop-gap for Hazard while I researched the High Fields, the place brought out a different side to her. Even with the wind and the rain, she always returned home flushed with something I couldn't quite identify.

I went up to meet her after class one time, and saw her teaching a group of schoolkids how to plant a tree. She was lost in it, the care, gently placing a sapling into a perfectly round hole filled with rich, dark soil. She directed the kids how to do it themselves, their careful placing and filling of soil mimicking her own. It was the closest I'd ever seen Hazard to being 'maternal'. I told her as much once the kids were all packed back onto their minibus.

"They're not so bad when you can give them back," she said with a wink. Though I noticed the way she diligently packed up the trowels and compost, the way she checked each of the larger trees on our way back down the hillside, the way she pointed out a shrike hunting for mice. I'd never known Hazard to 'love' anything, but that place came close. I was glad she was happy. It meant the slog would be easier for us both.

We worked together, me keeping up the grades and Hazard paying the bills, all while hunting for clues about a place we'd only ever seen in our dreams.

I found stories from the 70s about teens claiming an alien spacecraft had crashed off the coast, that they'd seen lights out there under the water. I found old newspapers from the 40s whispering rumours that Nazi or Russian subs were lurking in the area, and that you could hear the hum of their engines at certain points in the sea. Back further there were tales of the devil living out in the sea. Then a story of witchfinders come to the place to rid the area of pagans in the seventeenth century and throwing crucifixes into the water. I was thrilled to find a brief mention in a Roman centurion's message back to his family from around 300AD about a wild god of the Demetae people that lived off the coast of their camp. Even a piece of antler found in Torquay from when humans invaded and retreated from the British Isles over the space of thousands of years, enticed over the land bridge by migrating herbivores and beat back by encroaching ice. The antler bore a carving that looked somewhat like waves and beneath them grass and a dazzling sun.

Hidden away in background of history, all these stories corroborated our instincts, leading a breadcrumb trail back to the High Fields over and over. But no clues as to how to get there.

As for folklore, we were well acquainted by then with The Mabinogion *and the legends of Annwn. We found the High Fields' echo in tales from all around the British Isles. From the paradise of Avalon to the gateway to the otherworld on Tech Duinn, and even the phantom island of Hy-Brasil. But again, no clues on how to get there. Even* The White Book of Rhydderch *came up a bust.*

"The thing I don't get," said Hazard over dinner one night, "is what did Arawn even need Pwyll for anyway? Arawn is a king — he's immortal, knows old magic and stuff. What's he need some human for?"

"He wanted him to kill Havgyn for him and consolidate his power over Annwn."

"But why though? Why didn't he just kill the guy himself?"

"I don't think the story is exactly what happened." I pierced a piece of penne on my fork. "I think it's a metaphor. About power and faithfulness or something. The important thing is Pwyll takes Arawn's place. They swap positions. Arawn goes and lives in Pwyll's kingdom for a year and Pwyll takes Annwn."

"So?"

"I think this is saying that it's possible to not only visit but also to take over the High Fields."

"How though?"

"I don't know," I said. "I'll keep looking."

I filled out another request slip for the National Library of Wales. I'd been making my way through their Peniarth Manuscripts after impressing my lecturer in Medieval History with my enthusiasm. I was still accompanied by one of the library's conservation technicians, but she'd come to trust me enough to let me turn the pages myself—gloved, of course—as I made notes. I'd been after Peniarth 16 containing a collection of Welsh Triads—collections of history and folklore grouped in threes—from the thirteenth century. It was the oldest manuscript in the collection, and I'd had no luck getting access to it. Between lecturers, PhD students and other postdoc researchers, it was hard to justify letting an undergrad get time with the triads. So, when the conservation technician emailed me to come in and see something, I was expecting something special.

I wasn't expecting something from the turn of the nineteenth century.

I stood in the dimly lit viewing room in the bowels of the National Library, gloved hands hovering above yellowed paper, unsure whether this was some kind of elaborate joke.

"This is a new piece we've just acquired," the technician told me.

I kept my tone as neutral as possible. "What is it?"

"Let's see if you can tell me."

Ah, a teaching moment. It was amazing how often my lecturers and even the library staff would hinder my way so that I might 'learn something'. I hid my frustration and looked closer. It was paper, not parchment, and very neat, so probably machine produced. The writing was done by hand. There were four paragraphs. At the top of each were four lines of neat runes, though they included characters I'd never seen before. Underneath each was a translation in English.

"Triads," I said. "But I don't recognise the script."

"I didn't expect you would," she explained. "This was just discovered in a private collection. The owner died and left behind an impressive library of old manuscripts. We believe these may be some of the original notes from Iolo Morganwg's collection of Welsh Triads. He was an antiquarian in the eighteenth century. Then, in the nineteenth century, he

went full eccentric and became obsessed with Welsh history and mythology. Lady Guest even used some of his materials to help her translate The Mabinogion.*"*

OK, so more interesting than I'd thought. Then my eyes caught on the last triad on the page.

Three things which glitter and should be avoided:

The red-crested invader's sword

A Saxon's gold

The light under the waves of Dyfed

My hands shook. A new lead. I searched the strange runic script again.

"What was this translated from?" the question poured from me. "I've never seen runes like this before. How come none of the other manuscripts mention it?"

The lead technician burst into laughter. I frowned, confused.

"That script? It's Coelbren y Bierdd, or 'The Bard's Alphabet'. And it's completely fake."

I blinked. "What?"

"Iolo Morganwg was a notorious forger. Half of the triads he published he altered, the other half he made up. Including the Bard's Alphabet. Probably thought it would make his forgeries seem more authentic if he could claim the Celts had a unique pre-Roman writing system. He said they'd been carved on the four sides of a squared length of wood, hence the structure of the Triads: Intro, first item, second item, third item. Probably made them himself. He even claimed he was the last remaining bard of an ancient druidic order. Ran his own cult in London, doing rituals up on Primrose Hill. All reincarnation and ancient Celtic gods and what have you."

I must have gone very quiet because she suddenly changed tone.

"I thought you'd like it. What with your interest in Victorian neo-

druidism and pre-Roman mythology. I hope I haven't—"

"Did he ever admit to forging the Triads?"

"Of course not. He and his son Taliesin swore they were authentic 'til their dying breaths. But some people are like that. So desperate to have some sense of a pre-Christian Celtic culture. Strange, really."

I stared at the paper.

"Where was this private collection from?"

London. Of course, it had to be London. That night, I walked into the sea for the first time since we'd moved. I took it as a sign. But how on earth was I going to convince Hazard to up sticks and move again?

Looking back, I sometimes wondered what would have happened if she hadn't agreed to come to Aberystwyth with me. If she'd stayed living in her nan's spare room, built a life for herself back in Severn's End, maybe I would have lost interest in the High Fields, joined the other students and done normal student things: going out, drinking games, dating, study circles in the library, maybe making set pieces for the drama society. I always saw the other students laying out on the greens drinking their iced coffees piled with whipped cream, talking together and making plans, and I'd feel a pang of… something. But we made our choice. And you don't get to the High Fields without sacrifice.

Together we graduated with a first in Ancient History.

And yes, after graduation, I cut my degree certificate in two and gave half to her. She even framed it. My half's still in its tube somewhere, I think.

Fourteen

The Faithful retreated out of the sun and into their stone houses or under the shelter of the trees' parasoling shade with their humungous leaves. Part of me wanted to keep an eye on Peter and maintain some damage control, but I needed to talk to Her Highness. On the one hand, we both needed to be on the same page if we were going to keep the police off the scent. On the other, I needed to find out what on earth was going on with her and that...

The memory of her screams came to me, unbidden. *Don't leave me, Carys.* Bubbles in the rockpool.

I squeezed my eyes under my thumbs to make it stop. No, now was not the time for nightmares. Now was the time for action. I took off my shirt and tied it around my head to protect myself from the blazing sunshine, then headed out of the copse of cherry and apple trees and into the barley fields beyond.

The barley stretched before me like an undulating sea of gold. A welcome breeze skirted the tops of the glistening feathered heads, sending a shimmer rippling across the gentle rolls of hills and soft dips. The Faithful would head out soon to reap how many sheaves they felt they would need.

However, the barley seemed a little strange today, like it was larger somehow. I plucked an ear, warm and toasted by the sunlight, and took a closer look. The kernels had an irregular shape to them, like they were bulging from within. Closer to the top, some already had green tips peeking out of them, like they were already sprouting. I turned the ear over in my hand and a large flying insect crawled over my fingers. I dropped the ear, shaking my fingers. The insect took flight and landed on another nearby stalk. It was one of those wasps again. The parasitic ones. I knelt down to look only to spot another one crawling up another ear a few feet back. I straightened up and looked over the field. That hushing sound that I'd thought was just the breeze through the barley now sounded more like a soft buzz. The field was crawling with wasps. What were they doing in the barley?

I shook my hands again. I didn't have time for creepy insects. I continued on to find Her Highness.

The sky above was pale and hazy and bright, so you could never quite figure out where the sun was until it flashed right into your eyes. Sweat crept into the creases of my eyelids and beaded across my top lip, and the smell of toasted grass and dry earth rose up with the heat shimmer. Ahead I could see the bright curls of Her Highness, perched on a low hill under the shade of a blooming chestnut tree, its large wide leaves each a green umbrella, its dotted pyramids of white flowers swaying gently and pertly.

I trudged through the field, parting the barley with my hands, feeling the scratch and itch of the leaves and stems against my arms, trying to avoid thinking about the wasps.

I was glad I was wearing boots. In the past, Her Highness would part the barley ahead of us. The stalks would bend, as if to bow as she passed. I'd never thought about how hard it was to walk through the field before now. But on I trudged regardless.

I'm pretty sure I was interrupting when I arrived, but I didn't care.

"Your Highness." I lightly bowed. Better to go with deference after how badly our last attempt to talk had bombed. "Can we grab a moment and talk? There's something you need to know."

I stood slightly downslope from where Her Highness and Corin lazed in the shade of the chestnut tree, the bright blue sky stinging my eyes. Her shadow shifted and the smell of roses filled the air like strong perfume. Corin rested against the trunk with an arm obscured by the branches and the shade, presumably wrapped tight around Her Highness' shoulders.

"Can we speak in private?" I asked.

"Anything you want to say to me you can say to him," her voice murmured as if right next to my ear.

I noted that she didn't use his name. Perhaps she'd forgotten it already.

I flashed Corin a look.

"I think it would be best if we kept this between us."

"Wow. First you don't even think to congratulate me. Then you try to exclude the father of my child," she tutted. "Carys, I'm surprised."

"I'm…" Corin was sitting right there, watching me from the shade. I searched for the right words. "I'm happy you're happy—"

"You don't approve?" Corin scoffed.

"Thank you, dear heart," said Her Highness. "But there's no need to—"

"You don't get to approve!" he continued, rising to his feet. "Who do you think you are?"

"My dear," Her Highness said the words through a smile that looked more like gritted teeth. "I don't need you to defend me. It's not like *she* can hurt me."

"Of course she can't hurt you." Corin held her hand. "Who could? I knew from the moment I met you, you were invincible."

God, I wanted to spew. How was she stomaching this? He'd wormed his way in good and tight.

"But," he said, "that doesn't mean I like it when people try, when they think they can." He shot me a haughty look.

My cheeks burned. I swallowed back the urge to leave right there and then.

"It's important," I said.

The Queen shrugged. "Oh, if it's important, then of course. Let me drop everything." She sighed, turning to Corin, who shook his head in return.

"You'll see," she said. "It's always important. Everything anyone wants to say to me is important. I never knew there were so many dire things going on all at once until I became the Queen. No one ever told me anything important before. I guess they had been hiding it all when I was some nobody from Severn's End. All the important stuff out there. Mounds of it. It really has been very revealing. You'll see. Just watch."

I braced against her admonishment, teeth digging into the inside of my cheek. Where did she get off claiming herself a nobody? She'd been cock of the walk at school with her posse of hangers-on, copying her baggy jeans, her spiked hair, her homemade piercings. Now she was a Queen.

On the other hand, it was good to see the prom queen act slip a little, to see a little of her casual cruelty spill out. Her spiked brittleness. Hazard was still in there somewhere. Perhaps I could coax her out of this feminine-divine cosplay. Then maybe she'd start telling me what was going on here and we could fix our Peter problem and then I could leave, for good this time.

"Doesn't it worry you at all?" I indicated at her stomach. "After what happened the first time."

Corin's face didn't change, but I noticed his eyes dart to Her Highness. I could almost hear him thinking, *first time?*

"Why should it?"

Either she'd blocked out the fear and the panic of that strange day or she was pretending.

"Because," I lowered my voice, "this is what *it* wanted."

"*It?*" Hazard didn't share my interest in discretion. Her voice boomed. "There is no *it*. There's only me. I create."

A tree rushed up from the ground beside me, knocking me to the floor. It was a great grand oak, a rich vibrant green, each bough thicker than my whole body, its trunk like the leg of some great ancient beast, its canopy a small island, its branches rushing toward the sky as if it might embrace the sun.

"*I* destroy!"

With a groan, the tree's branches fell from its trunk like pine needles shaken from a Christmas tree. The oak tumbled apart, into logs, into splinters, exploding into a cloud of dust before it even hit the ground.

"It is gone. It is dead." And then darkly she added, "You saw to that."

I felt the words like a punch to the chest. The memory of bubbles in the rockpool, Common Brittonic chanted under my breath, my hands frozen by sea water. It came to me at night or at quiet moments. My burden to bear, I thought. We'd never really spoken about what had happened that day. I didn't think she'd…

"Hazard, it wasn't human."

She avoided my eyes.

"You believe me, don't you?"

Suddenly, the ground shuddered. The white flowers of the horse chestnut all fell in a single shower, while the pistils left behind swelled up into green spiked balls. The leaves of the chestnut tree started to brown, like rust was leaking out of the trunk and along the phylum of each leaf. A ripple of burnished gold spread out from the hill through the field, ripening the grasses and their seed until I could smell the barley malty on the air.

Her Highness doubled over, clutching her belly, her formerly silky brow now crumpled like creased linen. I froze.

No, not again.

"Motherfucker!" she said.

I stepped back from a sudden flood of fluid puddling into the summer-dry earth. Corin rapidly blinked in shock. He swooped to her side.

"Are you alright, my love—"

She hissed through clenched teeth.

"I'm going into labour, you daft fuck!"

Fifteen

Aberystwyth had run to the end of its usefulness. We knew a bit more about the history and shape of the High Fields, but nothing about how to get there and even less on what to do once we got there. I was convinced the missing information we needed would be found in London, in the lost Triads translated by Iolo Morganwg.

I'd searched through the Morganwg collection at the National Library of Wales and even made a day trip south to the Welsh-language school named after him in the village of Cowbridge in the Vale of Glamorgan. But they had nothing further on "The lights under the waves of Dyfed". The only option left to us was to hunt down the other manuscripts found in that private collection. At least that was the case I made to Hazard.

For the second time, Hazard's dedication to taking the High Fields wavered.

"You go," she said. "We've got the flat here. It's cheaper than finding a place with two rooms in London. And have you seen train prices? I hardly see nan enough as it is. She said something about her hip in her last letter. She was playing it down, of course. But you know my dad's terrible for checking in on her. I'll wait in Aberystwyth until you have what you need."

The idea of going to London alone terrified me.

"If you don't come with me, there'll be too much for you to catch up on," I said. "Too much you won't understand. I'd have to go to the High Fields by myself. We go together or we don't go at all"

I watched the conflict play out in her head over the space of a week. Each day she came back from the forestry with a face like thunder. Each morning she barely spoke to me over breakfast before disappearing back out into the trees for another day. I was convinced I was losing her.

Then, one day, she came back early and announced that she'd quit. Before I could ask anything, she dragged her suitcase out of the cupboard and asked when we were moving. I didn't question it, just quickly made the arrangements and tried not to think about what I'd made her give up.

I found an internship at an auction house for antiquaries in London; rare books and manuscripts. It wasn't like the plush auction houses for the more popular vases-and-paintings crowd, with their deep carpets the colour of money. No, it was the sort of place with original dark wood panelling, ancient brass light switches and old iron safe doors. The visitors were of the dusty academic type or the odd esoteric, hunting for forgotten tomes they barely dared to name in any volume above a whisper. My duties mostly involved manning the front desk on auction days and updating records, but thankfully these mind-numbing tasks I was overqualified for left plenty of time for checking past sales, of which there were plenty, though not very well-organised. I'd originally promised we'd be done in a year, but as I dug through the auction house's practically palimpsestuous records, it soon became clear that I'd been somewhat optimistic.

Unfortunately, though Hazard had half our degree on the wall of her room in our flatshare, she didn't have it in name. With no woodlands to help upkeep and my internship being unpaid, she worked in fast food joints during the day and in clubs at night to keep us afloat. Like at university, I was busy digging for information while Hazard took the brunt of real life. The grease, the general public, the grime and the noise and the whole world looking past her. Meanwhile I buried my head in the past, helping would-be sellers and buyers estimate values during work hours and searching through records of private collection sales on my breaks, hiding deeper and further from the present I'd never seemed to be able to bear but Hazard was now stuck with.

I didn't want to admit it to her then, but I was happy. I enjoyed this life, away from Severn's End, away from the pull of the High Fields, surrounded by artefacts of a lost past. For the first time, it felt like I belonged somewhere. My colleagues didn't push me to be more sociable, the work away from the front desk was interesting and my niche interests in folklore and mythology went down very well with the auction house's marketing department. They were always looking for tidbits to drive interest in certain pieces and apparently I had a gift for 'product storytelling', whatever that meant. They even offered me a paid position on the team, offering a starting salary worth more than what both of Hazard's jobs brought in together. I saw the hours the marketers worked and bristled at the thought of losing so much time for my personal research. I never told Hazard about it and instead quietly turned it down. I wanted to stay lost in my otherworld of artefacts and history. I didn't want to think about how miserable Hazard was here, about how I'd dragged her away from the forests she'd loved to a city she clearly hated. But there was no way I could have afforded the move without her. So, I kept my head down, focused on my work, stayed late and tried to pretend I didn't see the bags growing under her eyes, her skin growing dull, her edge crumbling away under the constant thrum and grind. I avoided her, not that she had much to say those days anyway. She just sat in her room and smoked while I sat in my room and read.

By the time I was offered a paid position as a trainee valuer we were barely talking.

I now made enough that Hazard could drop the fast food job, but *then our schedules were so mismatched we barely even saw each other. We passed like ships in the night, silently ignoring one another, focusing on our own lives. There were times when I was more surprised to see her at home than to come home and find her room empty.*

So it made it easy when, during my first month in the trainee position, I found a matching reference for the sale of the Iolo Morganwg manuscript to the National Library of Wales. There had been other items in the lot. And they were still in London, including a long four-sided wooden post of 'debated history' carved with runes that said something about the "Light of Dyfed". I printed out the details, then hid them under my bed in my room. I remember sitting on top of my duvet, aware of the hidden clue beneath me as if it was blaring like a lighthouse. What if this was the final piece? Was I ready for it to be over? To leave this new life I'd built? To go back to Severn's End? I decided to keep my discovery to myself until I made up my mind.

But then circumstances made up my mind for me.

Hazard got word—too late—that her nan was sick. And for the first time in years, we went home.

Sixteen

The Faithful came running through the yellowing fields to Her Highness' aid. I stood, scared and unmoving at the base of the hill, reeling with echoes from the past. I was back there, salt water on my face, biceps burning, palms stinging from the oars, as Hazard's moans reverberated against ancient stone. A rustling flurry of falling leaves broke me from the memory. The wind rose with Her Highness' labour pains, pushing me away, back toward the Hollow. I fought it for a moment, to be there for her, but I gave in quickly. I let the wind take me, stumbling along through the buffeted barley as leaves, twigs and seeds battered my back and the rising chill leeched the warmth from my bones. I put my shirt back on and went in search of the central fire, hoping to distract myself from the fear and the worry. I hoped she was right and I was wrong.

God I hoped I was wrong.

The Hollow was empty when I got back. The fire was out, and the stone huts were quiet. It was eerie in the early autumn colours without the quiet bustle of the Faithful. Especially now there were so many of them. It made the Hollow feel even emptier without them. How had Hazard and I lived here alone for so long?

Leaves littered the ground, yellow and red, where just this morning there'd been pink and white blossom. My eye kept catching on something, some detail in the world that wasn't right, that I couldn't quite put my finger on.

My stomach rumbled. I hadn't eaten since we set out in the boat this morning. I'd been so caught up in everything here I hadn't noticed. Perhaps a quick bite would help. One of the best things about the High Fields was the fresh harvest each day. The apple tree on the edge of the fire pit was drooping with clusters of russet red fruit, crowding out the browning leaves and bending the branches low to the ground. I detached one with a twist and took a bite.

Then immediately spat it back out.

The flesh of the apple was riddled with roots and leaves, as if the seeds inside had already germinated and were now trying to push their way out. I picked the bitter fibres from between my teeth. It was inedible. A careful search of the tree confirmed the rest of the fruit was suffering the same overgrowth. The skin of each apple was slightly raised with bumps and veins from the seedling within fighting to get out. Some already had buds pushing through the peel. Just like the barley in the field earlier. Everything was germinating too early.

I leaned close. There was that pattern again in the peel, the same repeating lines and spaces I'd been seeing all over the island. Only here they were cleaner, fresher. Two lines crossed by a smaller, like rugby posts, like the letter "H".

I pulled a leaf from the tree and looked at it closely. Instead of the lines of the xylem and phylum there were faint letters. A word. The same word. Over and over, making up the pattern of the leaf. I put it up to the light, hoping beyond hope. My blood ran cold when I recognised the word.

HAFREN

I looked at the stones running like a river through the Hollow, carefully tracing paths for the Faithful. On each, lines of sediment or fine crystals spelled out faint "Hafren"s.

Oh no.

The charcoal in the community fire pit was snaked with cracks in the shape of "Hafren".

No no no no no.

The wasp eating from my bite mark in the root-ridden apple, its iridescent wings a repeated fractal of "Hafren".

No, Hazard. What did you do?

I pulled my hand through my hair. The name was everywhere. The High Fields were riddled with it like termites. I bet if I dug down into the soil, I'd find it written into the bedrock, onto the very core of the earth itself.

"What's Hafren?"

Peter stood behind me. How long had he been there?

"Peter," I said. "Have you heard anything about the birth?"

"About that. Is she really pregnant?" he asked.

I rubbed my temples.

"It's… I don't have time to explain. Where is everyone?"

He tilted his head and put his hand to his phone, tucked into the front pocket of his jeans.

"Are they in danger?"

I hope not, I thought. Out loud I said, "No, I'm just…

I'm…"

"Feeling a little left out?"

In other circumstances I would have told him to fuck off, but that wasn't a bad cover. I shrugged, hopefully convincingly pathetic and petulant.

"Do you know where they are?" I asked again.

"Yeah, but there's something I want to clear up with you first, if you don't mind."

"Can we do this after I've—"

"Not really. See, the thing is," said Peter, "I spoke to April and June and they don't remember ever seeing any of the missing people. They don't recognise them at all."

I blinked, unsure what he was getting at. I needed to speak to Hazard. Find out what was happening.

"So?"

"So, you said you didn't recognise them either. You said…" he flipped through his notebook and read out loud, "they must have arrived after you left. But you also told me earlier that April and June arrived just before you left."

It took me a moment before I realised how badly I'd fucked up.

"I don't really understand the timeline here. I mean, June and April obviously recognise you. They welcomed you very warmly this morning. But they don't recognise any of the missing people. In fact, they say they've never seen them before. How could April and June not have seen any of these missing persons if they all arrived after you left?"

"I don't know; maybe they were on a different part of the island." I was reaching and I knew it, but I couldn't think of anything else. "Things have changed since I was here. I don't know how Haz— Her Highness runs things anymore."

He smiled without breaking eye contact. "See, I don't buy that at all. I asked the rest of the Faithful if there was another settlement and they said no. So, either your best pal has another island somewhere up her sleeve or," he put away his notebook, "you've been lying to me."

My fingers went numb. I could feel my heartbeat throughout my whole body.

"I think those people arrived while you were still on the island. I think something happened to them. I think *she* did something to them, and you couldn't stomach it, so you left."

Why? Why had I brought these men to the High Fields?

"And that expression tells me I'm right." He sighed. "Look, Carys, this will be much easier if you just tell me what happened."

"Easier how?" I asked.

He blinked, slightly taken aback. I don't think he expected me to ask.

"Easier than a whole squad of armed officers coming ashore. I don't think you want that, do you?"

I laughed, "That's the worst you can think of?"

He crossed his arms. He still wasn't getting it. The danger he was in just being here. He pulled out his phone.

"Fine, I'm calling it in."

"No! Wait, please, wait," I said, sweat running down my spine. "Let me talk to Her Highness."

"I don't think that's—"

"Please, just let me tell her what the situation is. I think I can convince her to get everyone to leave the High Fields, then maybe we can explain what happened. You saw some of the things she can do. That's not even the half of it. Trust me, you don't want her panicking."

He clenched his jaw, walked away from me, stared up at the crisping leaves, then returned to me and said, "You have an hour."

"And be careful what you say round here," I said.

"Are you threatening me?"

"No," I said. "Believe it or not, I'm trying to protect you."

"Funny," he said, "because it looks like you're just protecting her. Would she do the same for you?"

I wanted to hit him.

"An hour. Do we have a deal?"

I shook his hand. I had no choice.

"I saw a procession going into the woods back that way," he said. "If you're quick you might catch up to them."

I hurried away from him and into the trees. Now I just had to hope there was still enough of the old Hazard in there to hear me out.

Seventeen

It snowed the day of her nan's funeral.

"At least I don't have to worry about what to wear," said Hazard over her wardrobe of black. It was the first thing she'd said since finding out. She stopped going to work. Didn't even call in. Just sat in her room in our flatshare, staring at the walls.

We got to the crematorium back in Severn's End just in time for the service, riding all the way from the city in our most respectful black outfits. No one had offered a room for us, and we couldn't afford a hotel, so it had to be a round trip. The memorial garden looked like a black-and-white photograph in the snow. Even the order of service was monochrome.

Hafren Evans, *it read,* Beloved wife, sister, mother and grandmother.

I remember thinking how Hazard never mentioned her nan's name was Hafren. I wondered if it was an old family tradition or if Hazard's nan had intentionally been named after the beautiful, drowned goddess of the River Severn. Probably not the latter. I'd noticed how things like names trickled down the years, shedding their meaning with lost history. Anyway, it wasn't the right time to ask.

Hazard sat close to the front with her family. I was placed at the back with the well-wishers. It was strange to be separated. I'd spent so long glued to her side, it was odd to think of us as two separate people, with separate circumstances that didn't flow from our personal differences, but came from lives we didn't share. It struck me that I'd never properly met Hazard's parents. She talked about her nan a lot, but she never spoke about her mum and dad. To be fair, I never spoke about my parents either—what was there to tell? They wanted a certain kind of daughter and they got me instead. I continued to disappoint them like all children disappoint the unreasonable expectations of their parents.

I watched her family from afar, her dad sitting with crossed arms, looking anywhere but at the pulpit, an almost petulant refusal to engage with the grief of the moment. Her mum hunched over, swaying slightly, a faraway look in her red eyes. I thought perhaps the doctor had given her something, but the smell of vodka on her later confirmed that wasn't the case. Hazard sat between them, straight-backed, steady. I turned my eyes down onto the pale blue carpet. I'd always been happier as an observer, but this time it felt wrong, like I was ogling someone else's grief. I thought about what Hazard would see if she saw me with my family. What would she think? How would she sum me up looking at the evidence of where I came from? Then again, she'd probably never have the chance to. When the time came for a funeral in my family, my father would likely be sat on one side with his new wife and her golden-haired children, my mother would be sat on the other side with her new husband, fussing over the latest grandchild she so desperately wanted to mother, and I'd be sat on my own in the middle of the church, right in the centre of the aisle, a lost artefact of a family that stopped existing decades ago, like the bones of a long-extinct bird.

In the eulogy, the minister quoted a passage about a 'good woman' from the bible. How she gets up before dawn and stays up late to serve her family, how she dresses well, how she brings her husband only joy.

Later, as we met back up in the crematorium car park, Hazard paced and chain smoked, voicing her anger between puffs of cigarette, tipping ash into the gently piling slush on the tarmac.

"She was her own person!"

"I know."

"They made her sound like a robot."

"I know."

"Like she was just here for them."

"I know."

"Like her only fucking value was how useful she was to them."

"I know."

"She was the best of them. And they never saw it. She deserved better than that."

"She deserved better than that," I agreed.

Hazard threw her fag into the snow, where it went out with a short hiss. We stood in silence, listening to the wind in the bare trees above us. I watched her, waiting, unsure. I wanted to comfort her, but I didn't know how. I didn't know what it was like to lose someone like that. I tried imagining what it might be like perhaps to lose her, to try and empathise, but the resulting emptiness was too difficult to imagine.

Hazard stared into the grey slush, uncharacteristically quiet.

"I don't want to go out like that," she said.

I scoffed. "Like you ever could."

"I mean it," she said. "I don't want to go out like that. But," her shoulders slumped and she shrunk a little, "the older I get, the more I feel myself getting pushed into that mould. I work, but all my work is to clean and cook and smile. That's the worst part of it. The having to smile like everything's fine all the time. This whole world is a machine, pushing and pressing on us until we're too tired to fight anymore and we just do what they want. Be what they want. Clean restaurants we don't own, cook food we can't eat, raise the next round of workers and do it all

with a smile and a thank you."

She slumped onto the hood of a car, head in her hands.

"I'm tired, Carys. This world is trying to bend me and I'm fighting it, but I'm so fucking tired of fighting. But I'm so worried that if I bend I'll break."

I remembered the beach, the rum, the bracing wind off the ocean and the freezing sand under our bare feet, the fire dancing in her eyes as she laid out The Plan. She'd been there for me then. Now it was my turn to be there for her.

"Then let's make it bend to us," I said.

She looked at me.

"Did you find it?"

"Maybe," I admitted. "I think so."

She smiled for the first time in months. It was decided.

"In honour of Hafren Evans," she said.

"In honour of Hafren Evans," I replied.

We would take the High Fields. Or die trying.

Eighteen

I ran to the woods as the sun started to fall, setting the colour-show of leaves alight. Reds and golds saturated the crisping leaves, as if they'd been set on fire. The path through the forest led the way like a red carpet, or a trickle of blood. As the air cooled and the fields beyond yellowed, I kept thinking of Her Highness. I imagined the Faithful leading her, her strong arms draped over their shoulders. I remembered the weight of those arms across my shoulder, the way her knees buckled into grey grass and mud, her moans directed at the earth. I ran harder.

Leaves fluttered quietly through the golden hour light that filtered through the darkening branches in dashes and dots. The air was rich with the smell of leaf mulch and turned earth. Water seeped up through the ground, the mud sucking around my boots as an autumn mist crept through the golden ferns. It was almost as if the sea was rising back up from underneath us, flexing its muscles, telling us *I can take the High Fields back if I want to.*

I arrived at the clearing too late.

The Faithful were picking each other up from the ground,

pushing aside broken branches and sharing concerned looks. In the middle of them was a bed made of fallen leaves and moss and decorated with sunflowers, like something out of those twee paintings of fairies dancing with mushroom-hatted children. Just off centre of the bed was a shallow puddle of viscera splayed out on the rust-coloured leaves as if to scold the trees. *See*, it said, *this is what real blood looks like*.

April spotted me first.

"Carys," she said, "thank goodness you're here."

"Where is she?" I asked. "What happened?"

"Well, ah, Her Highness went into labour. It was very quick. I've never seen anything like it." April smiled, but her fingers fiddled with her tunic. I noticed for the first time that it seemed to be hanging a little loose on her bony shoulders. "I went to check her dilation, once I could convince—ah, the father to let me get close, but there were all these flowers in the way, with red and grey petals, covered in thorns. I tried to push through them, but they turned into the heads of dogs, snarling white dogs with red ears, and then they became birds, but birds that were only wings. Only they had tails like snakes. I thought, *she's given birth to some new fantastic creature*. But then they cried out, singing with men's voices, and melted into sea water. And there was a baby."

I braced myself.

"Was—" my voice warbled. I cleared my throat. "Was it alright?"

"*She*—until she tells us otherwise—looked just fine, from what I managed to see," April shrugged.

It looked fine? That didn't sound right.

"What about it's—her eyes? What were the eyes like?"

"Brown."

No coloured light? No distant stars circling in its pupils?

"And her cry? Was it—?"

Ringing like bells? Vibrating in your bones?

April laughed. "Well, she was making a fair racket, but that's normal after being ripped out of your comfy bed of nine months—oh, well, I guess it wasn't even nine hours. I guess Her Highness didn't want to wait around."

A baby. An actual baby. I'd been wrong. There was nothing to worry about.

Then why wasn't I relieved?

I'd half-hoped Her Highness was kidding. That the pregnancy was some convoluted joke designed to hurt me. *Look*, I'd imagined her saying, *I made my own family. Why would I need you?*

But the child was real. Human.

"Where is she now?" I asked, somewhat cowed.

"Her Highness scooped her up, looked at her, and then, before I could clean the wee girl, she clutched her to her chest and was gone in a flash of flame. Nearly took my tunic with her." She patted a scorched patch on her baggy clothes. I looked around at the remaining Faithful. I couldn't see Corin, the lying opportunist, anywhere.

"Where's Corin? Did he go with her?"

April grimaced. It was the face a well-meaning friend makes when the band they've come to support plays out of key.

"No," she lowered her voice to a whisper. "She left without him. I don't really blame her, to be honest. I mean, most partners struggle at births, but he was…"

"Insistent that he knew best?" I suggested.

April pressed her lips together into a hard line, either suppressing an ill-willed laugh or her honest feelings on the experience. Whichever it was, she soon gave in.

"He kept getting in the way," she said, "demanding he be allowed to see, questioning everything I and even Her Highness said, asking over and over about when he'd get to cut the umbilical cord. God, it was like he was obsessed! I almost told him he'd be wearing it as a noose if he didn't get out of my way!" She took in a deep breath and exhaled. "Her Highness should watch out for that one. I don't think he deals very well with feeling powerless. Not at all. But that's birth for you. No one's really in control. It's the body and the baby in the driving seat, and the rest of us are along for the ride. After that, I'm not sure how he's going to handle being the paramour to a god. He was pretty sullen after she disappeared. He went up to the Falls to find her with a face that could turn milk."

Ha, serves him right. Silly boy. But I knew that embarrassment deep down in my chest. The burning cheeks. Thoughts scattered like bowling skittles. When Hazard's moods took her, she acted fast and then you were stuck playing catch-up, trying to see the version of you she was reacting to, trying to find out what the you in her head did wrong now. Godhood never stripped her of her spitefulness. I wonder why I ever thought it would? None are more spiteful than gods.

June spotted us and hurried over, her tunic hanging about her chest like it never did before. She was nowhere near as stocky as she used to be. Come to think of it, everyone was looking a little thin. I remembered the apple back at the Hollow, and my mouthful of roots and leaves.

"April, what's happening with the food?"

She opened her mouth then looked at her wife. June, just arrived to us, heard what we were talking about, sighed and nodded.

"Every day food grows and ripens just as it did before, but lately..."

"They're sprouting early," said June. "Too early. At first it was just one in every dozen. Then it was one in ten. Then one in five. Over the last few days, we have to be quick if we're to get anything at all."

She held out a bag where she'd been harvesting tomatoes just before the birth had begun. Inside was a tumble of tomatoes, ridged with thick veins under the skin, pierced here and there with sprouting shoots.

"These'll be inedible now. We've been making do each day, but the sprouting just keeps taking over the rest of the crops."

"We don't want to complain," April's eyes shifted back to the others, "but people are starting to get a little grumpy."

A cold breeze rattled the fallen leaves across the forest floor as a cloud of those wasps gathered round the blood in the clearing's mossy bed. Their feeding made a low sickening hum against the gentle hushing wind. The branches above us were gently shaken of their crowning glory.

"How many boats do you have on the High Fields?" I asked.

April and June looked at each other, unsure, and then back at me.

"I think we have a couple," April kept checking with June.

"One or two might still be watertight."

"Do you think…" I thought carefully. How best to avoid a panic? "Could you head ashore for a few days?"

"Um, you mean me and June?" April cocked her head.

"She means all of us," June's eyebrows furrowed together. Her stare could have bored a hole through my skull.

April smiled like I was joking. "We can't all go."

"It's just for a little while," I said. "Until Her Highness and I can sort out what's going on with the food—"

"We're not going," June squared her jaw.

"It'll be alright, June." I put a hand on her arm and tried to direct her toward the Hollow. "Just for the night."

She pushed me off. It was the first time any of the Faithful had ever come close to laying hands on me.

"June!" April reached for her wife. June held her.

"I know how this goes. We leave for a night, and then the uniforms arrive and the tents are trashed and the yellow tape's put up and you've got to move on. I've seen it all before." June's eyes glittered. "You know, we believed in this place. An island protected by an actual goddess, not run by some slick asshole telling pretty stories so we'd live in tents and work while he luxuriated in his mansion on the hill. A place where we could live peacefully, not chasing after money until we drop. I'm not giving up on that. Not even for a night."

I couldn't help but stare. Hazard and I had had no grand plan for the High Fields. We were just two young women trying to make a home. It had always felt like we were the only misfits in the world, the only two people without a place, without an easy role to slot into. I'd never thought that the Faithful were the same, looking for a place to be themselves, to belong.

"Oh sweetheart," April cradled June's face toward her. "Oh my darling. We did that. We made it, you and me together. We'll always find places like this because we build them, together. As long as I'm with you, that's all I need."

June clasped April's hand close to her cheek, her breath starting to mist-up in the quickly chilling air.

"I just want you to be happy."

April shook her head, "You already make me happy. And we shouldn't base that happiness on the actions of someone else. Even if they are a goddess."

I watched the two older women hold each other. They looked like those trees you find sometimes that grow twisted around each other, wrapped together, so you couldn't think about chopping down one without also taking the other. I thought of Hazard and those nights on Abergafren Beach, the long rainy afternoons in Aberystwyth, the hot summers in London.

"Did she look OK?" I asked. "Her Highness. Did she look like she was alright?"

April and June gave me this strange look, like surprise slowly melting away into sympathy. They turned to each other and shared an expression I couldn't parse.

"What?" I shifted my weight between my feet. "Is she fine or what?"

"Forgive us, my dear," said April. "We just forget sometimes, what with how much you two achieved with this place, just how young you still are. How little of the world and yourselves you really know."

"You should talk to her. Really talk to her this time," said June. "I think she'd like that."

Nineteen

We pooled all of our money and our holiday leave and headed back to Severn's End. We'd hoped to use Hazard's nan's old place to stay, but her dad had sold it. Said it was to pay off the mortgage, but when we arrived in town we saw a new car in their driveway and both of them sported a fresh tan. I didn't really blame them. Money came along so infrequently in that part of the world; it was best to make the most of it before it was eaten up by life's misfortunes.

Hazard was less understanding. She went down to the house to see for herself and found it gutted, repainted and full of strangers. She hunted down her dad to find out where all her nan's stuff had gone. He said he'd sold the jewellery, but the rest had gone in the skip. Clothes, china, knick-knacks and all. Even the cross-stitch cat cushion.

"It was just old lady stuff," he'd said.

Hazard spent the rest of the afternoon in the pub, and I was left to set up at the caravan park on my own.

I rented us a one-bed holiday caravan on the cliffs above the dunes and beaches of Abergafren. It was a pale olive-green decorated with pink floral curtains and built-in furniture that was so tacky to the touch we had to cover everything with the spare bedsheets. It didn't come with internet access, so I had head out to the communal café and swimming pool to use their Wi-Fi, bracing through the wind and rain, sheltering my laptop under my coat. Sat in the tiled seating area overlooking the tiny pool and gym, I made a mental note of the rowing machine sitting idly at the back.

I logged in and got in touch with the buyer of the four-sided post carved with runes. Turned out to be The Museum of British Forgeries, a small volunteer-run kind of place enjoying a trickle of eccentric tourists exploring the back streets of London. The museum boasted a collection of terrible fakes and poorly constructed reproductions, including a poster of the Mona Lisa that had been pasted with egg whites and nearly duped an American oil baron. A polite email was all it took to get photos of the wooden post. I'd been tempted to take the train back and look at it myself, but photos would have to do.

It was about three feet long and two inches deep and wide, with four level sides etched with bardic runes. "A beaut of a forgery," the museum's curator told me. "You'd almost believe it was really medieval."

I imagined the feel of it in my hands, heavy and polished dark with age. Would I have immediately spotted it as a fake? Or would I have smelt the sea on it? Would I have felt some pull from it, like my connection to the High Fields, and know it was real? I sent the museum organisers a generous donation and offered them a copy of my translation after I was done. Hazard turned up in time to buy a bag of chips from the café before it closed and headed back with me to the caravan, passing the bag wet with vinegar and rain between us through the gathering dark.

I stayed up late with the photos of the post while Hazard slept off the drink. First I translated the runes into our alphabet, and then I haphazardly translated the ancient Welsh—or faux-ancient Welsh— into English. Hunched over my books, I couldn't sleep until I was done. By the time a groggy Hazard emerged from the bedroom in the pale light of the morning, I had a draft:

Three examples/guides/rules for holding/capturing/
owning the light of Dyfed:

A pursuit/chase in the spirit of Pwyll and the fair Rhiannon

A living emptiness in the spirit of Pryderi's crib/swaddling

An exchange in the spirit of Pwyll and Arawn, King/
Chieftain/God of Annwn

We cooked up some bacon and looked over it again.

"Is that how we do it?" asked Hazard.

"Yes. I think so."

"What does it mean?"

"I don't know. But we'll work it out."

Twenty

The Falls had frozen by the time I'd climbed back up the Mountain. My breath gathered in clouds in front of my face, and frozen leaves—still red and gold—crunched beneath my feet. This was new. I was used to the cycling of the seasons over the course of a day on the High Fields. Flowers for the morning, bright sunshine in the middle of the day, all the fruits and vegetables we could ever want in the afternoon. But winter? I'd never seen winter on the High Fields before.

The smell of snow hung in the air, briefly inspiring memories of picking out pine trees at the forestry. Pine wasn't native to Wales, but it had the right eerie type of beauty. Why had we never made a pine forest? Perhaps, once all this blew over, we'd make one that me, Hazard and her daughter could disappear into. The forces from the mainland would never find us in a maze of trees. We'd be safe. We'd be free again.

"She won't see anyone."

Corin's voice startled me. My eyes adjusted to the growing dusk, and I spied him, hunched at the edge of the Falls. A curtain of ice blocked the way into the cave beyond the frozen cascade of water. That was where Her Highness was hiding, and she'd locked him out. Good. That would make the conversation a little easier, not having to worry about who was listening in. Now we could talk properly.

"Head down to the Hollow," I said as I passed him. "They've got the fire going."

He stared at me, then laughed.

"What is with the attitude of you people?"

The comment caught me off guard.

"*Our* attitude?"

"Yes," he said, all seriousness. "I don't know what I've done to offend everyone here," he put air quotes around the word 'offend', "but there's been no reason for people to treat me the way they have. I was shoved aside at the birth of my own child. All my suggestions were ignored. They wouldn't even let me cut the cord. I don't know whether you know this—and it might help to get an outsider's opinion—but you all come across as very rude. And bossy. And…"

My mind filled in the blank. *Uppity*. I could have kicked myself. I'd come across lots of men like this in academia. I'd always ignored them. Their petty dick-measuring had felt insignificant compared to my research. This sort of casual misogyny was just another concern I'd planned to leave behind on the mainland. I should have twigged the moment he questioned my route to the High Fields.

"And now you come up here and think you can tell me what to do."

He crossed his arms.

I grabbed him by the collar.

"I was here before this mountain we're standing on even existed. The grass on this island regrows each morning and even that will outlive your stay. It is *not* your home."

My rage subsided and I realised the ridiculousness of what I'd just done. I wasn't Hazard. I wasn't Her Highness. I wasn't the Queen. I wasn't a god. I was just Carys Price and I'd barely made him hunch. He laughed at me. I hated the sound.

"Wow, you really think you're the only one who gets all of this," he said.

"Yeah yeah," I said. "PC Peter told me all about your sad little posts on The Queen's Court Forum."

Finally, I saw a flicker of anxiety in his smug face. The corners of his mouth twitched, and his pretty eyes searched my face for a hint of a lie.

"What?" I feigned surprise. "Didn't you know? He's a police officer. And he's been following you for some time."

Not exactly the truth, but close enough to be true. It was interesting to see how much the news shook him. Corin looked back down the Mountain, face set grimly, thinking quickly. Peter being a policeman worried him about as much as it had worried me. Whatever. I didn't care about his petty troubles. As long as they got him out of my way, that was fine by me.

"Thinking you shouldn't have lied your way onto the island now, huh?" I couldn't resist it. "Maybe you should have done the work and crossed the proper way, like everyone else."

"I still got here, didn't I?" He shot back at me. "Same as you. Same as her."

"Only because I brought you here."

"As far as the High Fields is concerned, I passed."

He looked at me now. It was probably the first time I'd ever gotten a proper look at him, without the dashing smile, without the charm, without the pandering, flattering, flirting gaze. He looked older than I'd given him credit. More serious.

"And for the record, I tried to cross the 'proper' way. I read. I fasted. I meditated. I went out into the wilderness alone. I opened my mind. I heard it calling for me. Like a keening in the heart," he thumped his chest. "I felt that call, like so many do. More than you see here. More than you could possibly imagine. And there'll be more still if the High Fields has its way.

"But when I tried to cross, the sea spat me straight back out. I thought the island was pulling a trick. Teasing, flirting, making me want something and then denying it to me. Then I found you and it made sense. Of course the High Fields wanted me – why else would I feel the pull? But it didn't want me honest. It wanted me something else. And now I'm here. Maybe you don't understand this island as well as you think you do."

He's a maniac, I thought. But there was an unnerving similarity to my own call from the island. I felt a looming dread that he could be right. I thought we'd tamed the High Fields, but I'd returned to find germinating food, fractal names and now a crossing that had become far too easy.

Corin swept his beautiful hair out of his eyes and composed himself. Then he stepped aside with a flourish.

"Go ahead. But she won't let you in."

I ignored him and walked up to the shell of ice capping the entrance of the cave. I put a hand on the ice, and it melted at my touch. I turned to gloat at Corin, but he'd already gone. With any luck he was making a hasty exit off the island and back into obscurity.

Good riddance, I thought and walked inside.

Twenty-one

We spent long days with rain drumming on the caravan roof, grey clouds looming over the sea outside, and steely waves rolling into the horizon, making cup after cup of cheap, grey tea and plate after plate of toast. We pored over my research and Morganwg's lost triad. I double-checked my translation with whatever guidance I could find online, but there was nothing to clarify its meaning, aside from the connection to the story of Pwyll.

The first part of the triad was easier to decipher.

"A pursuit in the spirit of Pwyll and the fair Rhiannon."

In The Mabinogion, *Pwyll sees a beautiful woman riding on horseback, but no matter how fast his horse gallops after her, he can't catch up.*

"Remind you of anything?" I said, nodding at the waves outside the window.

"Pwyll asks Rhiannon to slow down, and then he catches up easily," said Hazard elbows on the built-in table. "So, do we just ask to come ashore?"

"I think this is a parable on persistence and steadiness. But that's not a bad thought."

The last part of the triad was the most exciting element for us.

"An exchange in the spirit of Pwyll and Arawn, King of Annwn."

"They swap places," said Hazard. "Arawn takes Pwyll's kingdom, Pwyll takes Arawn's kingdom. That's what we want."

"They swap names," I clarified. "So, maybe when we get ashore we name ourselves the new king of the High Fields?"

"Who are we swapping with?" Hazard nudged me, "What if we turn up and we find Arawn there in his grey hunting garb?"

"I don't think Arawn ever actually existed. He's just a symbol of wisdom and power," then a little less seriously I added, "but if we see any white dogs with red ears, we'll just leave them be."

"But what if that's part of it?" said Hazard. "What if Pwyll wronging him was part of Arawn's plan all along? So he could trick Pwyll into doing his dirty work."

I ignored her and focused on the triad.

"The second part's the trickiest. 'A living emptiness in the spirit of Pryderi's crib'."

"Pwyll and Rhiannon's son gets stolen. Rhiannon gets blamed for it. Everyone thinks she ate him. So…" Hazard looked at me then back at the translation. "Do we have to steal a kid?"

I pursed my lips. Even after all the moving about, all the studies, all the sacrifices we'd made along the way, I had never considered how far were we willing to go for the High Fields. We'd never spoken about where we'd draw the line. It had always seemed obvious, until then. And The Mabinogion had a rich history of missing children, transformed children, unexpected children. Arianrhod was tested for her virginity by the wizard Math and immediately gave birth to twin boys. I tried not to think about it.

"I think it might be about a sense of vacancy. Pryderi wasn't dead, just lost. Also look at the repetition of "in the spirit of". I think this *is a mindset thing. Maybe that's what it means by a 'living emptiness'."*

"Maybe it's about being a bunch of lost kids," said Hazard.

We sat in silence for a moment. She'd been different since her nan's funeral. Every now and then she'd come out with some sudden brutally sincere statement like that one. There'd also been a definite uptick in her recklessness. She'd taken to cruising the pubs and bars in Severn's End late at night. I was never one to pry into her 'interests'; it just wasn't something we talked about. But after a string of mornings where she'd come back in the same clothes she'd left in the night before, I asked to make sure she was being safe.

"Why?" she'd asked at the time, "What's it going to matter once we take the High Fields?"

I supposed she was right. As long as it didn't get in the way of our efforts, what did it matter? But behind the partying, there was a sense of killing time, of spinning wheels, of finding small pockets of fun that would lead to nothing long-term. Neither of us were invested in our lives on the mainland anymore. We were both in a state of living emptiness.

I reached across the caravan table for her hand. To my surprise she didn't pull away.

"Well, if the High Fields is looking for two lost kids, I think we'll fit the bill."

I was convinced the High Fields were asking for a spiritual state of emptiness. I'd skirted around metaphysics during my studies, never quite interested enough to fully dive into that can of worms. But I knew where to get us started. I looked at comparative examples from around the world. Hermeticism, Buddhism, Kabbalah, Neo-Paganism, anything where people had supposedly managed to reach some higher state of consciousness. I built my knowledge of ancient rites and practices, and prepared to let the strange light of the High Fields take its place in my mind.

Each evening, after the day's studies were done, Hazard and I went down to the caravan park's café and swimming pool complex and got to work in the gym. We had to take it in turns on the rowing machine, but it helped if we competed against each other, seeing who could hit five miles the quickest, then seeing who could last the longest at the highest resistance setting. Hazard beat me every time, of course, but we both built up our arms and improved our stamina for the task to come.

In that rattling caravan park, we drew up our plan.

Twenty-two

Soft green lights led away from the frozen waterfall and down into the cave. I put out my hands in front of me, feeling for the cold damp walls, straining my ears to hear sounds of life ahead. Of all the places for a queen to reside, a damp cave was not one of the options I suspected most would imagine. Whether it was her cutting sense of humour or a dank and dark subterranean hideout, Hazard was always finding new ways to keep people at arm's length.

Down, down, down I travelled, until the cave levelled out and the light grew. I entered a large underground space. A ceiling of writhing green things shed light on the rocks below. Everything beyond that glow disappeared into darkness. At the edge of the pool of light from above, in a shallow shelf carved into the wall of the cave, was a bundle of cloth. The soft, delicate fabric looked like it had been torn from Her Highness' skirts. The bundle moved slightly. I cautiously approached. Here, up close, I could see how small it was, how vulnerable. Whatever fear I'd originally felt was swept away and replaced with shame. I didn't want to look at the child and yet I couldn't tear my eyes away, as if it would fall into darkness the moment I turned my head.

"What do you want?"

The Queen's voice, diminished somewhat, echoed from the darkness on the other side of the room.

"Your Highness?" For some reason I whispered. "We need to talk about something. It's important."

A shape in the darkness shifted. The Queen sighed. "What isn't?"

I peered, straining my eyes, trying to see her. "Hazard—"

"Is that why you came back?" Her voice was stronger now. Angry. Hurt. "Looking for favours?"

I bit my tongue.

"So what is it then?" she asked, "Cancer? Debt? Someone you love doesn't love you back?"

"There's a police officer. They're looking for some missing people."

Silence.

Her Highness stepped into the glow. She looked exhausted. Her face sagged and her eyebrows ground together like they'd been made that way.

"Are they on the island?"

I didn't need to answer.

"For fuck's sake, Carys—"

If the situation had been different, I would have been relieved to hear her curse my name, like I'd dropped wine on her favourite top or spilled coffee across our notes.

"I didn't know they were an officer at the time," I said.

"Is it Corin?"

"Pfft, no."

She tutted and turned. I knew what she was thinking. *Of*

course it wasn't Corin.

"Well, that only leaves one option, doesn't it?"

I crossed my arms. "Are you going to let him leave in one piece?"

"He's trespassing on *my* island," She stabbed her index finger in my direction, showering me with a small flurry of hail. "Meddling from the mainland will not be tolerated."

And yet he made it here.

"If you touch him, there'll be more of them," I said, brushing hail off my shoulders.

"And if I tolerate this *infringement*, there'll be more of them anyway!"

I lowered my voice. "They know he's here. If he doesn't return to them, or check-in after a while, the police will come looking for him."

"Then I'll build a wall of thorns and ice around the island."

"Then the army will come knocking."

"For one piddling PC Plod? I don't think so."

"No, for an unknown threat just off the coast of their territory. You know the only reason we've had no trouble so far is because no one in charge over there believes the stories from this place. If they knew what you can really do, do you think they'll just turn a blind eye? Do you want to take on an army?"

Hazard laughed, cold and dry, like the crunch of frost underfoot.

"Question is, does the army want to take on *me*?"

If I was honest with myself, I didn't really know who would win in a fight with Hazard anymore. With the increasing witness from the Faithful, there was every chance we'd yet to see the full extent of her power. But I was well-accustomed to her temper, and I knew if push came to shove, she'd watch the whole world burn before she gave up the High Fields. I had to try something else. Something drastic.

"You're not killing him and that's final!"

And then I punched her in the arm.

The Queen stared at me. She kept me waiting for five terrifying seconds. Then she clenched her jaw and threw up her arms. The cave rumbled and the worms above glowed bright like stars.

"You're such a stubborn cow! And it's never when I need you to be."

I held my nerve.

"I have to be stubborn. Because you're a temperamental bitch."

She shot me a look. Clearly no one had spoken to her like that in a long while. She sank and the floor rose up to meet her. I sat next to her.

"All those years," she said, "planning and scheming. Didn't plan for this, did we?"

I shook my head.

"We didn't mean to hurt anyone. We just wanted a place of our own."

"To be left alone."

"No career advisors telling you to become a teacher."

"No dinner parties where everyone pretends like they're so sophisticated just because they cut up a few sticks of cucumber and shoved them in a pot of hummus."

"No awful businesswear and leaning in and annual reviews."

"No diet chat and those little concerned looks and the whole 'oooh you should join my yogaaaa class. It's sooooo easy. Even yooooou'd like it, you lazzzzzy slob!'"

I laughed. I couldn't remember the last time I had. Probably the last time I'd been on the High Fields.

"Just being ourselves," I said. "No one trying to change us into anyone else."

"And if they come and try—"

"We don't let them ashore!" we said in unison.

"Fuck 'em."

"Fuck 'em!"

Hazard looked at me, smile fading a little.

"Why did you leave, Carys?"

"You know why," I said. We looked up at the glowing ceiling. "You could have come with me."

She waved me off. "This police officer. What does he want?"

"He wants to know where the missing people are. Their families are worried about them."

"Lucky them," she said.

"This is serious," I said. "If he doesn't get answers, he's going to come back with more officers. There'll be an investigation. The army might actually get involved."

Hazard laughed. "Good luck to them!"

"I told him I'd ask you about it. I was thinking I'd say they left. That you don't know where they went. We could blame it on religious differences or something. Whatever we say, we need to make sure our stories are straight. He's already caught me out once before. I don't want to—"

"You know my dad came once."

I sat upright. I'd more or less forgotten about our families once we'd taken the High Fields. Hazard leant forward on her knees and looked up at the glow-worms on the ceiling.

"I let him in. At least I think I did. To be honest, I don't know how much control I have over how people get here. More and more turn up all the time. Even he made it onto the island. Even though he didn't make it over by himself, even though he'd gotten someone else to row him. Even the waves were calmer so he could make it ashore. Last person I want to see gets the easiest ride in. Guess what he wanted?"

I shrugged.

"He wanted me to make a new liver for my mum. She was finally drinking herself to death. Silly bitch."

"What did you do?" I prepared myself for something bloody.

"Turned myself into an oak tree. Should have seen his face. He fell back onto his arse like in a Carry On movie or something." Hazard's face was hard to read. "I wanted to yell at him. Give him a piece of my mind. But I ended up just waiting for him to leave."

"Did he?"

"Not before taking a few branches. Maybe he thought he could sell them or something." She sighed. "He didn't even ask how I was."

Of course. What an idiot I am.

"How are you, Hazard?"

She looked at me and then her eyes darted toward the bundle on the other side of the cave.

"That good, huh?"

She leant in close, her voice dropped to a hush.

"All it does is feed and sleep," she hissed. "Feed and sleep. Feed and sleep. It's horrifying."

"Sounds like a baby," I laughed, relieved.

My comment did nothing to lighten Hazard's mood. She switched topics, slipping into something less vulnerable.

"You know what I miss? The forestry," she said. "It was so much easier there. Planting saplings. Taking care of the older trees. I thought the High Fields would be like that. Something that I could take care of. Something I could watch grow and feel proud of."

I twisted my hands together.

"I know. I feel so guilty about making you give it up," I admitted.

Hazard looked at me, frowned then laughed.

"What?" I asked.

"You think you made me give up the forestry job?"

"Yeah," I said, "when you came with me to London."

Hazard shook her head. "I went up for a promotion."

"You didn't tell me that."

"I wasn't planning on telling you squat. Like I wasn't planning on leaving," said Hazard. "But then I got passed over for the boss' nephew. I knew I had twice the experience that kid had, so I went and confronted my manager."

"God, he must have been terrified," I said.

"Yeah, terrified enough to admit they were worried about how committed I was," Hazard huffed. "Apparently young women don't stick around. They thought I'd been sprogging up in a year or so's time and then they'd have to fill the position again. Imagine that. Me. Back then. The maternal type."

I gawped. All those years. All that guilt. And it had never

been my fault at all.

"You should have said something. We could have fought it!"

"I didn't know that then. I was too angry. I just quit on the spot and left." Her eyes darted back to the bundle on the other side of the cave, "Sort of ironic when you think about it."

I nudged her shoulder with mine.

"Look," I said, "I'm sorry for doubting you, about the baby and all. I thought it was... y'know... like what happened when we first came here. I was just scared. But look, I was wrong. Everything's fine. And you're a mum now. For real this time."

But Hazard was shaking her head.

"I don't remember much from the day we came. But I remember seeing *it*. And I remember what you said about *it*. That it wasn't human. That it was just using us. But..." Her face froze.

I knew what she was seeing in her mind's eye. It was the same thing I saw in every rockpool.

"What if I was mistaken?" I finished the sentence for her.

I'd often wondered the same. More than I'd like.

Hazard continued. "I couldn't stop thinking about it. Its face. Its hands. I think that's why... I started having these dreams about my nan. At first, I just dreamt I managed to make it back in time, before she died. That I managed to say goodbye to her before she went. But then she started talking to me. Telling me how she wasn't really dead yet. That I had the power to bring her back. That if I just got a little bit stronger I could do it and everything would be alright again. It would fix the High Fields, make it behave, make the witness easier to control. It was just dreams, but it made me think, about other ways my nan could live on. I mean, why does anyone have kids, right? Some people do it because they're bored, or they're lonely. But I was doing it for her. And I thought at least a baby wouldn't just fawn over me like everyone else. She'd be like you. Like nan. Like family." She looked over at the wriggling bundle on the other side of the cave. "You tried to warn me. But I didn't listen. You were right. It's not human."

I felt the horror pooling in my stomach and creeping up my legs.

"No," I said. "She's human. She loves you."

Hazard shook her head so hard the curls practically vibrated.

"It doesn't understand love any more than atoms understand hope or planets know fear. It just is. And what it is, is hungry. And it wants me to feed it."

Hazard was scaring me.

"That's babies. They're hungry. We feed them. We teach them to love."

"Do we? Or is love just the thing we paint over the hunger? To stop us eating each other alive?" Hazard stood up. "This whole place, it does things, wants things. Like how more people keep turning up, like how I can't seem to stop anyone just turning up on the island anymore. It has a mind of its own. That's why it's so different from the forestry. I didn't realise until now. The exchange, it never finished. We just delayed it. And now it's consuming me, Carys!"

I should never have left. Of course she'd fold in on herself, surrounded by the Faithful, seekers and adorers with their take take take adoration, with no one who knew who she was before, knew the truth of what this land was. Was there any wonder she'd start circling in, in an ever decreasing, cyclical, regression of identity around this entity she now was and would ever be. And now I'd helped tip her over the edge. I should never have left her alone with this, to carry this burden by herself.

She paced the cave, fingers twitching in front of her.

"It makes my skin itch, like I can feel it all over me, pawing at me."

I got up and took hold of her shoulders.

"Hazard, it's gone. It wasn't human and it's gone. I killed *it*. If it ever was alive. If alive is something that meant something to it. Whatever it was, it's gone now. It's dead. It can't hurt us."

She stared at the bundle, her eyes wide with a horror I never thought I'd see in her face again. I looked at the bundle and thought.

"I could take her away," I said.

Her face changed sharply. "Like you did the other one?"

I swallowed. The same cold weight I'd be carrying around ever since we first took the High Fields raised its ugly head.

"No," I said. "I could take her to the mainland. Where she would be safe."

Hazard started shaking her head.

"It's OK," I said. "It wouldn't be forever if you didn't want—"

"No, you can't take it to the mainland. It's too dangerous."

The cave rumbled around us. The bundle squirmed, a small whimper escaping from beneath the blankets.

"You need to kill it, Carys."

That cold weight spread over my whole body. I dropped my arms and it was like watching someone else drop their arms. Someone else stepping away. Someone else fighting off the memories. Someone else being asked to do this horrible thing.

"I can't."

"Yes, you can." Her eyes pleaded with me. "You know you can."

Rocks fell around us. My heart thundered in my ears. Hazard didn't know how much I'd questioned myself over the years. Wondered if I'd just seen what I'd wanted to see, so we could take the power for ourselves.

No, it was to save her. *And there's no telling what it would have done if I'd let it live. What's done is done. It's over and it's best to move on and forget.*

That's what I'd thought. That's what I told myself. But some things never leave you, and all the magic in the world won't make up for it. I couldn't live with that doubt again. I shook my head.

"Just let me take her away."

I'd always been bad at predicting what Hazard would do next, but she was lost to me now. And it was my fault.

Hazard's expression went blank.

"If you won't, I will."

I didn't think. I just acted. I picked up the bundle and ran back up out of the cave. The Queen roared behind me. I was sure I couldn't outrun her, but I could try. I needed to try. I threw myself back up the stone-cold tunnel, holding the bundle gently in my arms, the writhing green worms blaring above sickly and neon.

I ran as fast as I could, not even checking what was in front of me, just sprinting and hoping I wouldn't run into a wall of rock. I made it to the top, my chest burning with the cold air as my heart drummed in my ears. Outside the cave, snow was falling. The lights of the Hollow glimmered below between the bare trees on the hillside. I panted long and loud. Maybe I could make it back to the dinghy in time to leave with the others. Maybe I could undo everything after all. I shivered and pulled the blanket around the baby in my arms. Something hard and sharp poked my hand from within the bundle.

Horror and curiosity wrestled within me. Something wasn't right. Slowly, with a shivering hand, I reached for the edge of the blanket, gently pulling it back, to see what Hazard had birthed.

A small skull stared up at me with its hollow eyes, a deep crack splintering up from the back. I was holding a bundle of damp bones, stinking of sea water, staining the blankets black.

I dropped the skeleton, tiny bones scattering and shattering into brown-black splinters across the fresh snowfall. I'd forgotten how small it was. I stared down dumbfounded at what I was seeing. I thought I'd buried it. Far from the cave. How had she found it? Or had it come to find her. Come to find me.

"What the fuck?"

Peter stood on the edge of the clearing, staring at the bones at my feet.

Twenty-three

It was dark when we set out.

We chose to leave an hour before dawn. We'd head out with the fishermen, hopefully mistaken for hobby fishers ourselves and not gather too much notice from the rest of the village.

We left the caravan and lugged our provisions down the hill to the docks. This time we were prepared. Waterproof sheets, rope, water purifying tablets, flint, torches, multi-tool, pocket knife, canteens, military-grade rations. Hazard knew what we'd need. And it's amazing what you can find online these days.

After I finished packing, I called the auction house in London to give my notice. I sent an email afterwards to make it official. Hazard had already notified our landlord in London that we wouldn't be back. They ranted something about money and losing our deposit, but we didn't care. We'd decided there was to be no life for us left behind when we got in the boat, no life to exchange when we took the High Fields. Just in case. That night, Hazard even burned her half of our degree in the caravan park's rusty BBQ pit. I watched her and she watched it curl and blacken in the fire, the ashes floating up into the air and disappearing into the dark.

However, I did catch her sneaking something into the bags when she thought I couldn't see. I took a look before we left. It was an old photo of her as a kid sitting on her nan's knee, colours dusty, edges soft with wear, matching round cheeks split with big toothy smiles. I put it back and said nothing.

We ended up hiring a rowboat from the same company that lent us a boat when we were sixteen. The older fisherman was nowhere to be seen, his son now in charge of the operation. I was almost disappointed to miss him. I'd wanted to see his face when he recognised us. It would have been good to catch some indication from his expression that his earlier criticisms had been addressed. Here we were, Pwyll in spirit, ready to walk into Annwn like we owned it. But life is rarely like the stories. We quietly handed over the deposit for the boat, took our life vests and headed to the water.

We took a moment on the quay next to the boat to eat a bit of breakfast and watch the sea in the dark. The water was quiet and black in the dock, but further out, beyond the open dock gates, the waves hushed and sighed. I thought about those early days on the dunes, watching the waves, making up what we thought the High Fields were like. Here we were again, a little older, a little less talkative, ready to see it for real. I'd lost my appetite and Hazard's had grown over the last month—we blamed the rowing exercise—so I handed her the rest of my bacon sandwich.

"Thank you," she said.

"It's just a sarnie," I said.

"No, for coming here, for giving up the job in London," Her eyes didn't leave the water. "I know how hard that must have been."

I thought of Hazard at the forestry in Aberystwyth. My mouth felt dry.

"Let's get going, yeah?" I said, and got in the boat.

Out of the dock, the sea was as sluggish and bad-tempered as Hazard had been recently. The waves rolled and pitched in the estuary, rocking our small boat while we set up our rhythm. I set the course, following the pull from deep in my chest over the water, then Hazard and I rowed in unison. The lights of land dimmed behind us as we set further into the sea.

After an hour, fog closed in and the tides turned against us, just like last time. I grit my teeth and continued to row as waves cut across the front of the boat. My eyes scrunched against the spray, but I kept my focus ahead. This time we wouldn't go with the waves, we wouldn't try to go around or speed up. We would be as Rhiannon from the stories, steadily cantering on no matter what happened around us. A large wave hit us from the right. Water crashed over the side, rocking us and pooling salt water around our feet. It would have been easy to panic at that point, to give up and go back. But we stayed calm like we'd rehearsed. We kept our focus on the rhythm and pull of the oars, on the sound of the waves hitting the front of the boat, on the heat coming from our arms as we steadily continued to row. We bounced along atop the waves, always on the edge of being tipped, tides turning this way and that and the fog now close and moving around us as if we were being spun about. But I could feel the pull of the High Fields growing stronger.

"We're getting closer," I said over the slosh and the heave. "Keep going straight."

"I'm going to be sick," Hazard murmured.

"Let's try the hail," I said. "Follow my lead."

And I started to hail the High Fields. We already knew English wouldn't cut it, but it took me embarrassingly long to realise that Welsh might not work either. Even old Welsh would be too young a language. We needed to go back to the older Brythonic languages from when the Celts first arrived in this part of the world. It had taken some quick studying and some favours called in from some connections in academia, but I'd managed to source a translation in Common Brittonic.

Hail Arawn King of Annwn. Here arrives your friend

Pwyll ap Annwn.

We chanted over the rising wind and the crash of the waves, hoping our pronunciation wasn't too off, hoping the names from folklore held a glimmer of meaning for what lay ahead. I'd made a lot of assumptions about the High Fields over the years. Now it was time to see if they were correct.

I was so focused on the chant and the rhythm of the rowing and the dull burn in my muscles that I didn't register the waves and the wind slowing. Not as if they were dying down, but moving in slow motion, like time was unspooling. The fog was close now, so we couldn't see anything beyond the edges of the rowboat. Then steadily, like a knife gently sinking into soft butter, our boat pitched forward.

Hazard briefly looked back at me, concerned.

I shook my head. Keep going.

And, with a few slaps of sea water, we dived down into the murky waves.

I don't know whether it was the chanting, the metaphysics prep or just the exhaustion, but neither of us properly remember the descent down. Hazard saw a galaxy, a sky full of ringing stars through which we rowed. I saw a darkness, cold and silent, filled with grey weeds knotted with old bones. I don't know how we were breathing, let alone how we were moving through the water, but we kept rowing and chanting, down into the depths, gliding through our disparate visions as if on a voluminous grey mist. No matter how strange things were, I was filled with a glorious thrill, a perfect crystalline joy. We were doing it! After all this time, all the planning, all the dreaming. We were really doing it. It was real. We were right.

A light glimmered in the dark below us. As we drew closer, the light glowed brighter and the pull in my chest grew stronger until it was a powerful ache.

Grey grass slowly waved around the edge of our boat and in the distance—I think, distance was hard to judge—the shadows of columns upon columns rose up into grey, watery mists. Nothing moved as it should. All the perspectives were wrong. It was disorientating. If we hadn't wedged into something soft and wet, I doubt we would have known we'd hit the bottom. Land.

Ahead in the grey murk was a small hill surrounded by those towering columns. And in the centre of the columns was the light. The Light of Dyfed.

Hazard turned round in the boat to look at me, eyes wide. We silently grabbed each other's hand. We'd made it. But there was no time to lose. We got out of the boat and hoisted our rucksacks onto our backs. The weight of the packs was strange here, both buoyant and heavy enough to unbalance us. It didn't help that the ground was always slightly further away than we thought, causing us to stumble and wobble on our feet. The weeds and the columns shifted in and out of focus, like perspective and distance were shifting. It was like being drunk. Hazard and I threw our arms over each other's shoulder to help us stay steady, swaying with the weeds. The ache of the pull throbbed in my chest.

"We're so close," I said.

"Hold on," Hazard said.

All we had to do was endure it, endure the environment until we got to the light and could make the exchange. We staggered up the hill with the columns, edging toward where the Light of Dyfed pulsated with sound and colour. Up close, I could see the columns changed shape and style as they rose. Higher up they were smooth and pale, further down they had grooves and were made of sandstone, further down still they were made of gold and decorated with ornate fans studded with emeralds. At the bottom they were rough-hewn monoliths of bluestone, a ring of standing stones.

Hazard braced against the closest pillar and pulled me up beside her. I leant against her, catching my breath. The pull was so strong now and walking had been like wading through thick mud.

"Are you ready?" she asked.

I steadied my breathing, trying not to think about what air there was down here. Once I felt balanced and calm, I nodded.

We stepped into the stone circle. And we stopped.

For all of our talk of Arawn. Of Rhiannon. Of Taliesin. Of Ceridwen. Of lost Celtic gods. We'd always thought they were metaphors. Ancient archetypes guiding us toward hidden power. We never really believed in them.

And we never expected to find that… thing… there.

Twenty-four

"Where did those come from?" Peter pointed at the bones in the snow, "Is that—?"

April and June came rushing up the hill behind him.

"Carys," said June. "I'm sorry. We tried to get him to—"

Peter spun round on them, eyes turning back and fore between the women and me.

"What is happening here?" he demanded.

"Are those bones?" asked April.

I was frozen, both figuratively and literally. The air was so cold. Had winter always been this cold, or was it just the High Fields?

"I don't think you should—" June put an arm around her wife.

I broke out of my shock and clumsily stood in front of the bones, a bit too late now, and did my best to obscure them.

"What is that, Carys?" April asked.

Peter stared at me, furious, determined.

"They're just…"

Animal bones. A lamb. We found them here. They're the bones of an alien thing we found here that had died long ago.

A thousand lies played their way across my tongue, but the air to breathe them into the world failed to come up from my chest. I was tired. So tired. There had been so many lies.

A rumble from the Falls behind me shook icicles from the branches. Shards of ice rained down on Peter, April, June and me. They all raised their arms to protect themselves from the shards. I didn't. Hazard was coming. She would not be pleased to find Corin had abandoned her. Not after I'd left her too. Not after everything. Not now with this. Not with this ghost child at my feet. This dead. This wraith. This spectre at the feast, pointing her tiny just born finger.

Cracks spread through the frozen topcoat of snow.

"We need to go," some still sensible part of myself managed to speak, barely above a whisper. "We all need to go now. It's not safe here anymore."

It never was.

Peter pulled out his badge and a set of cuffs.

"Carys Price," he said. "You are under arrest."

June's face turned serious like a slab of granite. April blinked as if stumped by a crossword clue.

"What for?" April asked.

"Obstruction of justice, failure to disclose vital evidence and suspicion of murder of twelve missing persons," his eyes shifted to the bones hidden poorly behind me, "and one unidentified infant."

I crossed my arms behind my back. All the fears and the tension washed away. I never thought I'd feel relieved to be arrested, to be found out. But I was. It was over. I would leave this island. Everyone would have to leave. I would be put away. Safe. We would all be safe.

If only I could convince Her Highness to come quietly.

She burst from the cave mouth in a flurry of snow. Ribbons of ice cut crystalline paths through the moonlight, silver and cold. The frost hissed at her feet and her curls framed her face like a mass of writhing snakes, vivid against the white and the grey and the black of the evening around us.

"Where is she?" her voice shook the branches and cracked the ice over the waterfall, sending a shelf of frozen water sliding toward our feet.

June and April clung to each other. Peter marched toward her.

"No!" I leapt in front of him, facing Her Highness, hoping to bear the brunt of her wrath.

There was no explosion of power like I was expecting. No crack of frozen tree limbs and ice. Instead, there was a soft, wet *shunk*. And then a horrible ripping sound, as Peter's stomach was split right open.

Twenty-five

It was old, older than anything I can think of. And unlike anything I'd ever seen, not in all my research, not even in the dreams that had haunted my nights all those years.

It shifted and broke and came together again, rolling in on itself over and over, like a motorway tied in knots, eternal and yet always changing. It hurt to look at it, my mind struggling to make sense of what I was seeing, like a Magic Eye puzzle that only revealed itself if you squinted just right. All around it, stone was shifted into water, water into dust, dust into air. Matter bent to its whims like light bending through a prism. This was the source of the strange-coloured light. This was the source of the pull.

And it was… alive.

"What the fuck is that?" said Hazard.

"I—"

But before I could answer, it started to hum, as if whirring into life. The shifting, knotted pattern sped up, and the flashes of light, twisting and turning as if beaming from those hidden prisms, started to flicker and blur. The ringing sound upped in pitch and the standing stones echoed its song back with low, almost human voices.

"Shit," said Hazard. "Make the exchange!"

I snapped myself out of my stupor and focused on the task at hand. Hazard and I stood side by side, each raised our right arms, palms facing the undulating knot of light, and chanted in Common Brittonic:

Hail Arawn, King of Annwn. Put your form and semblance upon us and send us to Annwn in your stead.

The ringing grew louder and the ground beneath us shook. The grey grass billowed around us as if buffeted by a hurricane as the light flickered faster and faster. And in the flickering I saw movement.

"Carys, is it working?" Hazard called over the noise, eyes squinted near shut.

But I was too focused on the light to answer her.

In the flashes of light, I saw a story of stars, then ice then water then sky then ice then water then sky. And then in ice and sky people arrived from the East, and then there was water and they left and then there was ice and sky and then the people returned again. And so they came and went like the tides until one day the ice disappeared and the people stayed. And with the people the light grew in strength. Two men swapped faces and then there were miracles. A woman rode upon a horse that could not be caught. A man shapeshifted into a frog, a crow, a chain, an iron in a fire, a horn on a stag. A woman spontaneously gave birth to twin boys, and one became a rock and the other dived into the sea and became a wave. Giants danced in a circle on a hill. And then the giants became stone and then the stones were stolen away into the East. And then there was water again. And then there was war. And then there were new symbols. And the people's language changed. And the stories of miracles were still told but no longer understood. And then it was dark. And the light slept. And then there was a glimmer of a woman in aristocratic Victorian dress, poring over manuscripts. And then multiple new ears heard the stories and the light whirred back to life. And then there were fishermen and dreamers in a small seaside town. And then there was a girl who would look to sea. And the longer she looked to sea, the stronger the light grew. And then there were two girls, and the two girls grew, and the light grew stronger singing to them in their sleep. And then the girls were women and they were rowing and then they were here and they had brought a living emptiness with them and the light was strong enough now and ready to live again.

"Carys! Carys!" Hazard shook me to my senses. *"Carys, what do we—"*

The knot of light spasmed and the space in the centre of the pillars was thrown into a strange twilight. The grey water above turned a dark indigo and the ringing stopped. Then the knot came apart, a star unravelling like a jumper, and streamed into Hazard.

Over my years of study, I'd made a lot of assumptions. I'd assumed the figure of Arawn was a metaphor. Like I'd assumed the "emptiness in the spirit of Pryderi's crib" in Morganwg's lost triad was a metaphysical requirement. My instincts had been dulled under layers of knowledge. And all the while, Hazard had been asking the right questions. What had Arawn needed Pwyll for?

I realised too late that it wasn't an emptiness in the spirit the triad had asked for. No, it was a little bit more literal than that.

Hazard was also a little late in realising something.

She'd later tell me she thought it was the rowing practice or the grief over her nan or the pressure of what we were attempting to do. It wasn't only her that missed it. We'd both shrugged off her lethargy and her increased appetite. Turns out morning sickness doesn't happen to everyone.

Hazard stumbled back. Her hands scrabbled for the edge of her sweater. She wrenched her top out from where it was tucked into her trousers. Her lower belly shone with that ringing, coloured light. And then suddenly it started to swell. She clutched my arm, in pain and now *frightened of what we'd stumbled upon.*

"Carys! What is it? What's happening to me?"

Her stomach grew again, and she collapsed to her knees.

"Carys! Do something!"

I was frozen in terror as I watched her stomach swell. I should be doing something, I thought, but all I could think was, Why hadn't I seen this coming? *Arianrhod. Ceridwen. The Mabinogion was full of stories like this. What had I done to us?*

Hazard gritted her teeth and clutched the ground. The skin across her stomach writhed and squeezed. She gripped my ankles.

"Please," she cried, "don't leave me!"

Her stomach contracted. She screamed. I gripped her hand and tried to hide the fear in my face. She writhed and panted. Her spare hand fumbled at her trousers. I wordlessly helped her peel them off her clammy skin as my ears rang with her cries.

Light flowed from her like a river.

I turned away from the sight. Hazard was shocked silent. I'd never seen her look afraid before and it terrified me.

"Carys, am I going to be OK?"

I should have told her she was Hazard, King of the Punks, forest survivalist, the strongest person I'd ever known. If anyone could survive this it would be her.

But I didn't. My mouth dried up and I couldn't meet her eyes.

The stones around us rumbled. Hazard arched her back and screamed. The light burned bright and blinding. I ducked my head to the ground.

I heard the sounds of her pain, the grey water rushing around us, and then a ringing like broken glass.

When the light dimmed and the sound abated, I opened my eyes.

We were back on the surface. The strange marshland had risen above the water and the dawn was gently lighting the mists. Those impossible pillars had collapsed and lay in ruins arounds me, the stone slowly disintegrating into the mud. The air had settled and the water was still, like a mirror stretching out into the unending fog. The grey grass had wilted and was rotting to sludge. Whatever had been was gone, the banners burned, the castle torn to the ground, making space for something new.

Hazard lay on the ground in the centre of the marshy island and between her legs there was movement.

I got up too quickly, slipping in the mud and back into a rockpool, soaking my clothes. I clambered out, more cautiously this time, and picked up the creature from the ground. It looked human. Swung its small fists, scrunched its face and rooted around like a human. But when it opened its eyes, I swear I saw that light glinting those strange colours. And when it opened its mouth that ringing sound came out instead of a cry. I held it out at arm's length.

What had Arawn needed Pwyll for?

Iolo Morganwg and his druids had believed in reincarnation. And Arawn had used Pwyll to consolidate his hold over Annwn by taking his semblance. I didn't understand it all completely, but I knew the mewling creature in my arms wasn't human.

Hazard peered up at the creature, her eyelids heavy, her breath short and sharp. Then her eyes rolled back and she passed out, face drawing pale. There was a lot of blood. I put the creature down on the mud and tried to stem the flow with my jacket and her trousers, but it soaked through. I looked out over the water. There was no sign of land or any vessel through the mist. We were so far from help. Nothing but a miracle could save her now.

The creature screeched for my attention. It looked bigger somehow. Was it growing? I thought of Pryderi, Rhiannon and Pwyll's fast growing child. How long before this creature was fully grown? How long before it went looking for a kingdom to rule?

I knelt in the cold disintegrating grass, frantically thinking through the old stories, looking for a clue that could save us, save her. And then I told myself a new story, an idea, a solution to both problems at hand.

I made my decision. I picked up the creature, found a rockpool, took the gamble and did what needed to be done.

Hail Arawn, King of Annwn. *I said as I waited for the bubbles to stop,* Put your form and semblance upon Angharad Evans and send her to Annwn in your stead.

When it was over, there was a moment of stillness. Then the light ran in ribbons up through my fingers and over my arms, slow at first as if resentful, like it knew what I'd done. Then it rushed to the next living emptiness, left behind by itself.

After the light settled, Hazard opened her eyes. She groaned and it was the best sound in the world.

"Am I alive?"

I knelt beside her, tired, soaked through, shivering, trying not to think about what I'd just done.

"Better than alive," I told her.

She got to her feet, clothed now in that coloured light. About her head it danced and sang, morphing and changing, iridescent, all twisting colours and sound, her eyes shining with distant stars. She watched the light dance over her skin as she caught up with what had happened.

"How do you feel?" I asked.

Hazard breathed in through her nostrils, then exhaled. A wave of green rippled out from her, covering the mud with grass. The island pulled itself up out of the sea and the water retreated. Clouds peeled back and light and colour filled the air. The world bent around her. Finally.

I laughed. Partly from relief, partly from the joy of having done what we'd set out to do. It was ours now, and so much better than I'd dreamed. We'd done it! It was worth it. Everything, every sacrifice. It was all justified now. It would all be worth it!

I turned to Hazard, waiting for some wisecrack or another miracle just to show off.

But she was looking at the ground where the rockpool had been, her face radiant with that light and hard to read.

Twenty-six

Peter's face opened in surprise as his lower abdomen spilled his intestines onto the ground. He stared at them, as if embarrassed, like he'd dropped his shopping. He briefly tried to gather his escaping innards into his arms, as if gathering up scattered oranges and apples from a split plastic bag, before slumping onto the dirt.

Corin stood next to him with a knife.

Corin was bloodied.

Corin was smiling victoriously.

"He knew too much. And the ritual asks for an emptied living thing," he said. "Two birds, one stone, right?"

People still dream of the High Fields. And in dreams it calls them to it.

April rushed to Peter's side while June watched, her hand over her mouth. Corin threw down the knife with a dramatic flourish. Her Highness stared at him, snow and ice dripping from where her raised fist was frozen in the air.

"What did you do?" she asked.

He rolled his eyes at her question.

"Oh, come on," he said. "Not very smart for a god."

I could smell a shake-down.

"What do you want?" I asked.

Hazard's eyes flit to me. Corin turned my way and took me in. It was an awful feeling, being drunk in like that. Like being looked over for a meal.

"Was it a toss-up between you who would take it?" he asked. "Because I reckon miss dowdy here would have done a better job of it."

Hazard did not rise to the bait.

"Answer her," she said.

"I just want the same thing as you," Corin said. "I did the numbers on life. I saw the meaninglessness of it all. I walked around pretending that football and Christmas and weddings and births mean something when nothing means anything, just like you did, right? I found a community of like-minded men, just like you found each other. Then we heard about a strange island off the coast of Wales where miracles could happen, just like you did."

A sensation like cold water crept up my legs. Corin wasn't just a lazy aspirer to the faithful. He was something else. Something far worse.

"And we've decided to take it. Just like you did."

Her Highness visibly bristled, her soft dewy skin pierced now with spines and thorns as rage creased her face into a snarl.

"You can't take shit from me. I am The Queen!"

Corin smirked.

"No," he said. "You're just the vessel. You can be replaced."

Corin ripped open his shirt, revealing his chest scarred with random ogham, elder futhark and... was that from the lesser key of Solomon? I would have rolled my eyes and told him to go back to his drinking buddies at the lodge, if he didn't then pull out a phone.

"I came to put that power in the right hands, where it belongs," he said. "But then when you chose me out of all the others, I thought maybe there was another way. Regime changes can be so violent – perhaps a union would be better. And what better legacy than a child. But then you just had to cut me out when you were done with me. Typical." He shrugged. "So it's back to Plan A."

He thrust the phone up into the air. My eyes widened.

"I'm live streaming this back to my team and they're going to spread it all over the internet. Unless you concede the High Fields to us."

Oh Christ, I thought, *a 4chan hermetic order.*

All those times I'd worried that someone would try to take the High Fields from us. The police. The government. Another seeker. Now he was here. And worse, he was full of entitlement and empty of reverence for the danger of this place. He smiled, cocksure in his victory. We'd all been doomed the moment I'd set foot back on the High Fields.

I turned to where April and June were tending to Peter, their arms covered with blood, their faces aghast. April had torn a strip off her robe and was now pressing his innards, clumsily, back into the new cavity in the centre of his belly. Peter stared at the sky, face pale, eyes pulled wide, chest fluttering with sharp, shallow breaths. I pulled off my jacket and helped tie it around his middle. It wouldn't do much for long, but it might free up one of April's hands. She would need it.

"There's a dinghy," I told her, "close to the Hollow. Gather as many of the Faithful as you can and head for Severn's End. The tide will carry you."

June curled a hand round the soft flesh of my upper arm.

"We can't leave Her Highness," she said.

"She won't be alone," I said. "Take him and go."

June opened her mouth to argue, then looked at the light crackling behind me and then looked at her wife. I'd wondered at times, despite the professed devotion of the Faithful, where Hazard and I really ranked in their priorities. I was glad to see it was not as far up as I'd feared. June helped her wife to her feet and then the two women, strong and determined, hurried, carrying Peter between them, back down the hill.

Gods were to be run from; they'd learnt that from us at least. Too bad I hadn't learnt a thing. I turned back toward the crackling light.

Twenty-seven

When the first of the "Faithful" turned up, we hadn't known what to do. They came ashore on a child's inflatable dinghy, drifting through the fog like ghosts. Three of them. Instantly outnumbering us. We worried they'd come to claim the High Fields too. After all, if we could figure out how to take it, what was stopping someone else from repeating the ritual and taking it from us? The mists and the tides had protected us so far, but now with newcomers on the island they didn't seem quite as impenetrable as we'd once thought.

Those first few months we had been two Eves, building the island to suit our needs, picking out names for a whole new world, a whole new way of being. And after everything it had cost us to get here, we weren't about to give it up.

We made a plan. I'd talk to them—I'd always been the least threatening—and Hazard would overwhelm them with her presence and between the two of us we would convince them to get off of our island without any violence. But when they spotted us, when they spotted her, they dropped to their knees. We thought they were trying to hide at first, badly, but as I inched up to them, I saw they were bent over, faces pressed to the ground. I recognised what they were doing before Hazard did.

They were worshipping her.

I approached them carefully, mindful that they could be crazed zealots of the Kool-Aid cult variety. There were two men and a woman in the group, all wearing what looked like second-hand jumpers and old waxy raincoats, stinking of sea water and grass.

The woman among them, Mair, in her fifties at first look, not that much younger than my parents, carefully approached me in turn.

"We're here for her," she explained. "We saw this place in a dream. We saw her. A real-life goddess. We had to come."

Mair was from Cardiff. A bit far to be having dreams of the High Fields, I thought. But then the two men with her, younger and nervy, had also dreamed of the High Fields and they were from Worcester. Their dreams had started not long after we'd taken the island, like our presence here had erected some kind of psychological radio tower, boosting the signal further afield.

"The world's a mess," said Mair, "and it's not getting better any time soon. Anyone with sense can see that. No one knows where to go, what to do. But in the dream, I saw this place and I knew I'd be safe here, with her, the Queen of the High Fields."

It was the first time anyone had ever referred to Hazard as the Queen. She'd had a good laugh about that when I reported back to her.

"Fuck it," said Hazard. "Let them stay if it makes them feel better."

They'd been willing and able to tackle the mists and waves that shrouded the High Fields from the shore. They had earned their place here.

For a while they were little more than a curiosity to us. We'd never set out to start a commune or a religion, so the worship icked us out a bit, but they were harmless enough.

Then Hazard started getting… bigger.

She'd always been taller and broader than me, but where my eyes once met her nose, they now reached her lips, then her chin, then her collarbone. Her shoulders and hips widened, as if she was preparing to carry the world.

But it was more than that. She was also getting stronger.

Her 'powers' took less effort, were more effective. She could grow a tree in seconds, shape a hillside in minutes, flood a valley with rye with the stamp of her foot. At first, I thought she must be getting better at it, being a god that is. But as her skin glowed brighter and her eyes shone with increased internal fire, we put two and two together and realised it must be the newcomers. Whatever power the High Fields had given her, it fed off of them.

"Should we be worried about this?" Hazard asked me once. "What if the exchange—"

"No," I said. "The exchange worked. Not as we planned, but we're here, aren't we?"

"But I'm not controlling this."

"You're just figuring out how all of it works," I said, excited by the possibilities, keen for there not to be any problems.

She taught the Faithful how to light fires and how to build huts and let them get on with whatever it was that worshippers wanted to do. Sometimes they'd ask us questions, or—more specifically—ask her questions. The usual stuff like, "What happens after we die?" and "Why is evil allowed to exist?" Truthfully, we had no idea. The only thing we'd ever figured out was how to take the High Fields. If we'd been interested in anything else, did they really think we'd be here? We fumbled a few answers and tried not to think about how little we understood. Least of all about the High Fields themselves.

Twenty-eight

By the time I'd set April and June back down the Mountain with Peter, Corin had caught up on the situation and was now quickly seeing how badly he'd underestimated the Queen's power. I'd read about gods turning fleeing girls into trees before. I'd never imagined how horrific that would have been to see.

Foam ran from Corin's twisted mouth, pushing its way up his distended throat, long and gnarled now like the branch of a fleshy tree. His beautiful eyes bulged out of his skull as leaves pushed out from under his eyelids and buds burst through the skin of his cheekbones. Strangled screaming rattled from his chest as it grew and the skin split. He was conscious for far longer than I would have expected. At some point he'd either soiled himself or the changes to his body had squeezed the waste out of him like he was a tube of toothpaste. I stood watching, unable to do anything as his body twisted out of all recognition, fighting the rising urge to vomit. Her Highness blazed with uncontrollable virulent growth. His phone sat secure in the calcifying claw of his hand, outstretched. On the other end were a half dozen small squares, each a picture of a horrified face. I tried to reach for it, to switch it off, to stop feeding the divinity now blazing off of her like she was a nuclear reactor. But it was too late. They were already streaming the horror around the world.

"Hazard, help me turn it off!"

But she wasn't paying attention to me. She was looking at the small broken skeleton on the ground.

The bones shone white, burning their image in the back of my eyes. I shielded my face from them, hoping we'd caught it in time, hoping Corin had taken the brunt of his foolishness. But the damage was done. The crackling divinity was showing no signs of abating. Her Highness was staring at the bones, transfixed. As the bones glowed brighter, I thought of the name threaded through everything on the island, and I knew what she had done.

"Hazard." I squinted between my fingers, light burning my eyes and my skin. "When we first came here, when that thing came out of you... did you name it?"

Her boldness faltered, a fracture in that blazing confidence, grief and terror bleeding through the gap.

"Hazard," I begged, "please—"

"She deserved better. You said so yourself after the funeral," said Hazard. "You know she sent me letters while we were in Aberystwyth. And in London. There was a fiver in each one of them. No matter how old she got or how little she had, she was always looking out for me. Even when I didn't want it. She was there anyway." The ground cracked around her. "But they didn't even tell me she was sick until it was too late. I wanted to be there for her, and I couldn't because they didn't tell me. And then they gutted her house, and sold her things, and binned everything else. They threw her away like she was nothing. They made it like she had never existed. She deserved better. She deserved a legacy."

I knew what I should have said back then. When the Queen, when Hazard had asked if love was *just a thing we paint over the hunger*. I should have told her that I knew love was real because of how much I loved her.

But I hadn't.

"When I saw it was a girl, I realised she had my cheeks, her cheeks. So I— I couldn't help it. I just looked at her and I knew that was her name."

"Don't say—"

"Hafren."

The air exploded with light.

Twenty-nine

After centuries of obscurity, the High Fields were being noticed again. The more powerful Hazard became, the more people came ashore, the more powerful Hazard became.

There is power in being seen. And I liked it.

But I didn't like how crowded it was getting. There were only twelve of the Faithful at the time, but even that felt like too much to me. We were always interrupted for one reason or another, and it wasn't me the Faithful wanted to speak to.

I can't remember how I justified it. I think I thought if Hazard got powerful enough, she'd be able to perform better miracles, heal people, feed everyone, live forever. Maybe we'd be able to protect the High Fields from anyone who'd want to take it from us. Maybe I just wanted the satisfaction of being the one to share, to be the one who passed on the wonders of our world. Or maybe I just wanted to syphon off more 'witness', grow her power, without having to host more people on the High Fields, without having to share it, to share her.

Whatever reason I told myself, I made my decision.

One of the Faithful had brought a polaroid camera with them ashore. A trendy trinket that went with their overall vibe of LED fairy lights and dried flowers. They would probably have given it to me if I'd *just asked, but I didn't want anyone knowing what I was doing. I snuck it out of their hut and took a photo of Hazard, radiating that coloured light. The film didn't really do the sight justice, but it was good enough. And not something that could have been doctored with this kind of film. I went to the edge of the High Fields, slipped the photo in a bottle and set it out on the sea.*

Of all the things I've done—taking Hazard away from her nan, making her give up the forestry job she loved, hiding the final piece of the High Fields puzzle so I could stay in London, killing that thing that came out of her—this was my smallest, most thoughtless crime. And yet it was the one with the largest cost.

There is power in being seen. And the High Fields ate it up.

I knew the bottle had been found the moment I woke up a few days later. It was quieter than usual. The air felt still and empty, like walking into a family home and instantly knowing everyone else was out. No one was in the small circle of stone houses in the Hollow. No one was washing or bathing in the river. I thought of the photo in the bottle, then I went north to the lake where I knew Hazard often met with the Faithful, anxiety tightening in me like a violin string.

The lake was already gone when I arrived. Hazard was there, but she'd changed. Her hair had grown out and her body was thicker, taller. She towered over me now. Behind her, where the lake had been, the faithful were gathered in a massive writhing mound. Their bodies were swelling, their mouths hung open in wide awful smiles that ripped and pulled and sagged, voices raised in some ringing song. Or were they screams? Their mass grew and swelled into a mountain of flesh. Just thinking of all those limbs engorged and coagulated together, the eyes in enlarged pores, that wet old smell, makes my head swim.

"What did you do?"

"Nothing!" Hazard held her hands up. "I swear. I don't know what

happened. It just came out of me all of a sudden."

The witness had snowballed out of control and erupted Hazard's divinity into virulent growth, blossoming the land and the water and the Faithful like a tumour, until both earth and skin split and ruptured.

"I couldn't control it," she said. "It's like it had a mind of its own."

We locked up that part of the island, set it apart with thorns and cliffs. I'd have put an angel with a flaming sword there to guard it if I could.

I didn't tell Hazard what I had done, but any time she used her power after that filled me with dread. Did we really know what we were playing with here? Perhaps we should reassess what we knew about the High Fields, about her powers.

But then more people arrived.

April and June turned up on a summer evening when the golden light hung heavy like syrup in the fog Hazard had let hang for a week after the event. They came in a kayak, paddling together in perfect harmony, as they did in everything, dressed in wetsuits and not much else. I begged Hazard not to let them through, but she was hard to talk to. She'd withdrawn into her caves—a new addition she'd thrown together in the fog—and I barely saw her if it weren't in falling leaves or sun-flares or flurries of snow. I wished, and not for the first time, that I had her power. So I could make a wall of ice to keep everyone out. To keep them safe from us. But I didn't have her power. All I had were my words.

I went down to the shore to meet them. I planned out what I'd tell them on the way. I would tell them that the Queen had assessed them and found them wanting, that they had failed the test of initiation and had to leave. I hoped shame would be enough to convince them.

But when I arrived, I saw Hazard welcoming them, her arms wide open, her hair outshining the setting sun on the horizon.

She was different from before. She wore a flowing dress like a fairy princess and her hair swayed around her like she was underwater. Dreamy, ethereal and graceful.

She'd become the Queen of the High Fields. And what is a queen without subjects?

I stayed a week—or what passes for a week on the High Fields—to help the new Faithful settle in and work out maximum occupancy limits to keep the witness in check, then one morning I took their kayak and quietly left.

I couldn't do it anymore. After everything I'd done, everything that came back to me in the darkest hours of the night, I couldn't stay. I couldn't face another mountain of flesh, another rockpool of bubbles. So, I chose what I thought was the lesser evil.

I left her.

Thirty

Hazard's curls flew around her head as if in slow motion as light spiralled in ribbons out of her, eyes, fingers and toes. The ice on the Falls behind her evaporated. The tree that was once Corin fell to the ground. And that high-pitched ringing sound filled the air until it rattled my bones and shook my teeth.

When we'd taken the High Fields from the thing that presided over it, we were supposed to have named ourselves as its new gods. But when it had all gone sideways, I made the exchange to save Hazard's life.

But I'd only delayed it.

Whether she had meant to or not, that day in the weeds and the stone pillars, she'd already named a new god. She'd named it after the one person she'd ever felt truly loved by. She'd named it after her nan. And now it was ready to complete the exchange.

I'd let Hazard down so many times: when we went to London, when the god of this place took her for its own, when I left her alone with the High Fields to be devoured, but not this time.

As Hazard's divinity burst out of her, I ran forwards and threw myself around her. I locked my arms in place and I shouted over the rushing wind everything I should have told her long ago.

I told her she was Angharad Evans, the baddest, boldest person I ever knew. I told her she was the first person who ever made me feel seen, who ever made me feel like I mattered. I told her that the time we hitchhiked to Bristol to see a band, only to find we'd come on the wrong date, was still my favourite day. I told her that all those hours we'd wasted hanging out on the beach, mitching off classes, bored out of our skulls, were some of the happiest memories of my life. I told her that she was my best person. I told her how much I hated leaving her. I told her I'd come back for her. That I would always come back for her. That I was holding onto her, that I was never letting go of her, that I would hold on even if it meant the end for us both. That where she went, I would go too.

I kept holding on as screams filled my ears and smoke filled my lungs and blood in the air filled my mouth. And that colour, like light passed through innumerable hidden prisms, leaked through the skin of my eyelids. I may not have been able to see what was happening, but I heard enough to know the High Fields was burning. It was devouring everyone left standing. It was over.

Before the blast threw me to the ground, I thought of April, June and Peter. I hoped they'd gotten away in time. I hoped they had survived.

Then everything went dark.

I don't know how long I lay there, arms thrown over my

head, but by the time I came to, the High Fields had been reduced to ash. The trees and hills and fields were gone. Even the mountain of bloated bodies had been wiped away. There was nothing but grey sky raining ash onto scorched earth. I clutched my chest. Everything that was hers was gone.

An inhuman sound croaked from my split mouth. I'd never known a world without her. Even before we spoke, even when I'd left the High Fields, her presence had always been there. And now she was gone. What was I supposed to do without her now?

A wail carried on the wind, ringing like a thousand tiny bells. I stopped crying at the sound. It was coming from where the waterfall had been.

There, in a hollow of ash, no longer just a pile of old bones, a glowing thing squirmed. Its arms writhed and probed around the edge of its burnt crib, every inch of its flesh now iridescent with that strange light. Its fingers and arms grew long and looped back in on themselves, turning and knotting just liked I'd seen that very first day on the High Fields. I watched it in empty resignation.

I thought of Peter's wasp on the slug, of the ancient peoples who'd approached and retreated back and fore with the ice ages, of the exchange between Pwyll and Arawn. I'd been so confident that the thing that had ruled this place was dead, that we'd killed it. Instead, we'd incubated it, nurtured it. All those years after our arrival, it had been collecting power from us, from the people who were drawn here. Little by little, it had fed from us just as we had done from it. We'd never been more than a convenient host. A change of skins. A human Pwyll doing the bidding of an immortal, omniscient

Arawn.

And now it was ready to rise again above the waves.

In the smoke, embers were shifting, dragging themselves together. The burning trees were stretching new, thin limbs up to the burning sky. It was rebuilding already.

I staggered to my feet, intent rising in me. I let the memory came back to me.

I'd drowned Hazard's first baby in a rockpool. Her second wouldn't be so easy. But if I was quick, maybe I could make it sleep again. Perhaps that would be enough.

I lifted a rock, still hot from the fire, and raised it high above my head. Sometimes I wonder if the right one of us ended up being the vessel. It needed emptiness. And who was more empty than me? Perhaps I should have been the one to let the High Fields consume me. Perhaps it had.

I brought the rock down. Then I lifted it and brought it down again. And again. And again. Until that writhing, wriggling thing was still and lying in the ash.

I knew what would happen next. The sea would rise and the land would crumble and the High Fields would sink back down into the depths of the Celtic Sea from where we'd called it up. To die, to sleep, I didn't know. I gave the island to my god, to the ocean, to swallow it whole and keep it down in the depths of its belly, held tight by the endless crashing of the waves.

As the water started to rise, I picked up that thing and walked into the waves, like I used to do in my dreams all those years before. For some reason the sea had always kicked me back up to the air, to the shore, to life. I guess the weight of me had never been enough to take me under. This time it would stick. The thing in my arms, the things I had done, the things I had won and lost, these were exactly the right weight.

The High Fields sank back under the waves. Grey water climbed up over my legs, my thighs, my belly, my chest, rising over my collarbone, creeping up my neck. I felt the cold seeping into my legs and my arms as the water came up over my mouth. I closed my eyes, clutched the god of the High Fields to my chest and let the water take me.

The ashen earth fell away from under my feet. The light grew faint, and the water pressed into me firm and cold as I started to sink into the bottomless dark, the unending ocean. A stream of tiny bubbles fluttered up over my cheeks, my eyelids, my hair. I wondered how long it would take to drown.

Something grabbed the back of my shirt.

Sound, a voice, muffled by the water, came from above.

"Car...rys... Carys..."

I turned my head to the voice. A shadow dappled on the surface above me.

"Let... go.... Let go..."

But if I did that, wouldn't it come back? Another thing that was my fault?

And how would you stop it if you're already dead?

"Carys... let it go..."

I dropped the thing from my arms, letting it fall away, letting it sink back where it came from. Without it, I floated up to the surface, pulled by that fierce grip at the back of my neck. I was hoisted onto a thick, splintered tree bough, still boasting a few horse chestnuts. A firm hand whacked my back and I coughed up salt water.

Hazard leant over me, smaller, not glowing, un-god-like, face smeared with ash, ringlets melting away from her scalp and leaving only a dark stubble of hair. She balanced precariously on the floating bough.

"Oh, thank fuck."

My heart ballooned in my chest.

"Hazard!"

"Blew me clear across the waterfall." She wiped her eyes. "When I came to, you were walking into the water, like the first time I ever saw you. I thought I was watching you die that day. I thought you were gone."

I shook my head, tears hot on my freezing cheeks.

"Still here. You always said I was a stubborn cow."

I don't know whether she laughed or sobbed.

I reached out to her, like I always have done, like I always will. With one strong pull, she brought me up onto the bough with her and, shivering, we watched the High Fields sink around us. The waterfall, the Hollow, the river, the mountain of flesh now nothing but flaking ash. It all sank under the waves of the Celtic Sea. And far beneath us, the strange-coloured light, twisting and turning as if on hidden prisms, grew dimmer and dimmer as it descended into the gloom below. But as it sank, I noticed something. The pull in my chest didn't point toward it anymore. It never would again.

It pointed to the woman next to me, holding onto the bough with me for dear life.

It pointed to her.

Acknowledgements and thanks

The version of *The Mabinogion* used as reference for this novella is the 1997 Dover Thrift Edition of Lady Charlotte Guest's translation and introduction as published by J. M. Dent & Sons, Ltd., London, 1906.

Thank you to Harriet Hopkins for being one of my first readers. Thank you to Ms Evans and Mrs Jones for all the early encouragement. Thank you to Gavin Inglis, Ali Maloney, Josh Holton, Jane McKie, S K Farrell, Bram Gieben and everyone at Writers Bloc for all your feedback and patient mentoring over the years. Thank you to Abigail Pelik for (quite literally) keeping me sane. Thank you to Ely Percy for showing me how it's done. Thank you to *Shoreline of Infinity*, *Monstrous Regiment*, *The Selkie*, *Hedera Felix*, *Gutter Magazine* and everyone who makes the Scottish lit scene what it is today. Thank you to Francesca T Barbini for giving this strange tale a home. Thank you to Alex Davis for the kind editorial work. Thank you to Marit Hartveit and Helene Cloete for all the emoji 'spells'. And, of course, thank you always to Dale Peet without whom none of this would be possible.

And thank you to you, the reader. May the pull in your chest always guide you to safe waters.

Discover Luna Novella in our store:

https://www.lunapresspublishing.com/shop